I0773138

THE PSALM OF ASHEN SILK

Printed in the United States of America
First Printing, 2025

ISBN 978-1-960411-17-4 (eBook)
ISBN 978-1-960411-18-1 (paperback)
ISBN 978-1-960411-19-8 (hardback)

Published by Night Muse Press
Edited by Spencer C. Huff
Illustrated by Nathan Hansen Illustration
Stepback art by Sovana Arts

ACKNOWLEDGEMENTS

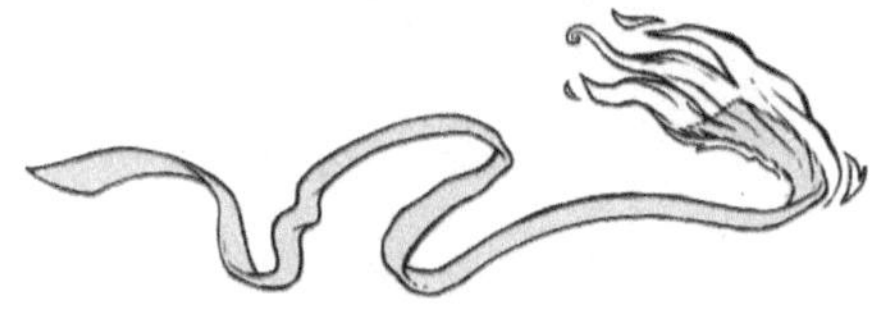

To my husband, Spencer – Thank you for your unwavering love and support, and for lending your sharp eye to this manuscript. This story is better because of you, and so am I.

To Cody – Your chaos is a strange and wonderful comfort, and you always make me laugh, even on the hardest days.

To my readers – Thank you for begging for more of this world. It is a joy and an honor to write it for you.

And finally, to Claude and Esmeralda – Thank you for showing me the beginning. For trusting me with the story of how your love first took root, and how your journey began. I can't wait to see where you take me next.

ALSO BY R. L. DAVENNOR:

The Curses of Never Series:

A Duel with the Dragon

A Dance with the Devil

The Serpent and the Swallow

A Land of Never After

A Sea of Eternal Woe

A Forest of Blackened Trees

A River of Tormented Souls

The Phantom of Notre Dame Series:

The Psalm of Ashen Silk

The Hells of Notre Dame

The Masque of Crimson Shadow

The Spectre of Moonless Night

Others:

Dragon Lake: A Swan Lake Retelling

CONTENT WARNING:

This novella is a dark sapphic romantasy intended for mature adult audiences. It contains explicit sexual content, graphic violence, on-page self-harm (related to religious penance), religious trauma, and the off-page murder of a family (including children). The story explores themes of systemic persecution, obsession, toxic relationships, and includes depictions of gender dysphoria and body dysmorphia

BEFORE YOU BEGIN:

This novella is a prequel to *The Hells of Notre Dame* and can be enjoyed either before or after the main series. It is a complete story that details the beginning of Claude and Esmeralda's relationship.

This novella is not intended to be historically, geographically, or socio-politically accurate to the period in which it is set. It is a work of fantasy fiction set in an alternate universe similar but by no means identical to our own, and as such, many liberties have been taken.

A note regarding Claude's identity: their label would be a nonbinary lesbian if they lived in modern times, but they do not have the vocabulary or understanding to reflect that in their current state. Their arc is an exploration of gender identity and how it shifts given one's surroundings. Instances in which Claude refers to themselves with gendered terms, both masculine and feminine, help illustrate that as understanding evolves, so does confidence. The correct pronouns for Claude are either she or they—though given her masculine presentation, note that there are also instances in which Claude allows themselves to be referred to with he/him pronouns both for safety and comfort. This character's experience is entirely fictional and is in no way intended to reflect the experience(s) or identities of real-life nonbinary or transgender people, though it is loosely based on the author's own experience. Queer people are not a monolith. One person's identity or experiences can be completely different to another's, yet both are valid.

Please also note that while Claude and Esmeralda are only involved with one another for the entirety of this book, they enter a consensually polyamorous relationship in which they are both permitted to seek out other partners of various genders, and will do so in subsequent books in the series.

Thank you, dear reader, for giving this story a chance.

I. THE CONFESSION

Claude

Father Laurent was late.

Or perhaps I was early, too anxious to pay proper attention to the time. I counted my heartbeats, then the faint tolling of Notre Dame's bells: two quick pulses, a hush, another two. Quasimodo would be up in the belltower now, serving his afternoon shift before being released to spend the evening with me. It was that knowledge alone that kept me from spiraling.

"Bless me, Father, for I have sinned." The hollow words caught in my throat. My existence was perhaps the greatest sin of all, but that was why I was here—to pay my penance any way I could. Inhaling deeply, I willed my racing thoughts to be still, fixating on the mesh of the confession booth grating.

The door creaked open, and whether my flinch was from surprise or anticipation, it was hard to say. Father Laurent settled on his side with the weary resignation of a man who bore daily witness to Paris's most abject failings, and I was one of them. The curtain between us fluttered, the scent of Laurent's pipe tobacco mingling with the incense residue seeped in the wood.

"Speak, child," he said at last.

I bit my tongue, tasting blood, and recalled the progression of sins I rehearsed. Not the *real* ones, of course. The safe ones: pride, envy, anger.

"I… I have harbored thoughts again," I said, and Laurent exhaled through his nose.

"Of what nature?"

Ah, yes. The familiar test of concealing the truth in acceptable words. "Of the flesh," I said honestly, and wanted to die from shame. Just this morning, I shooed the choir woman I took to my bed last night from my chambers mere hours before dawn. "I have tried to fast, but temptation—"

"Temptation is a demon with many faces," Father Laurent interrupted. "Do not think you alone are plagued by it." His tone was cautious, as if the devil himself had rules for how much sympathy to extend to a creature like me. I clenched my fists, feeling the crisp edge of my sleeve against my knuckles.

"Go on," he prompted, quieter. "What do you wish to confess?"

What I wanted and what I should confess were two entirely different beasts.

I *should* confess that every Friday, the moment the cathedral's shadow swept over the river Seine, I returned to my office and locked the door, letting my mind—and too often, my hands—slip into forbidden territory. I *should* confess that my thoughts of The Embermage had grown more obsessive, possessive, and lustful. I *should* confess that every waking moment, I pictured her captivating smile.

And God, I wanted—I wanted her so badly it hurt. I wanted to touch, to taste, to let her devour me—if that's what she wished. I envied the way she commanded a crowd with nothing but a flick of her wrist, her confidence, her laugh. The Embermage's very existence was so at odds with my own, yet it made me wonder what it would be like to break free. To leave behind the doctrine and vows by which I lived my life, and step out, wholly myself, into the world.

Such want was not just dangerous. It was impossible.

Even still, I was exhausted from running and hiding. What if I forced Father Laurent to hear the truth of the sins that ruled me, and what my devilish desires led me to do, time and time again? Would he listen, give me penance, or throw me back onto the streets right where he found me? Worse—would he reveal me as the imposter I was, humiliate me for all to see?

The implied threat was more than enough, so I held my tongue, as always. Inhaling deeply, I searched for the most innocent confession I could muster, uncaring that it still damned me. "I attended the street faire again… despite your warnings."

A soft click of Laurent's tongue, which may as well have been a slap to the face. "We all have our weakness for spectacle, Claude.

Was it the show or the performer?"

"The Embermage," I admitted. "She… she does things with fire I cannot explain. It isn't all trickery, Father. Sometimes… I think it's beautiful."

At least it was something resembling the truth. I confessed as much before in a gentler fashion, but this time, I let my sharper edges show. Laurent's sigh was long, the air between us thick with tension as he, too, seemed to choose his words carefully. I braced myself. Would he do exactly as I feared?

"Claude," Laurent said at last. "Do you know why the Church forbids such displays?"

Because they remind men—remind women—*of what could be, if only they cut their tether to society's rigid expectations. Because beauty, free of such constraints, is dangerous. Because God says that fire belongs to the devil, and those who wield it are his brides.*

I'd never fully believed such nonsense, and I believed it even less now. The Embermage's latest performance remained as vivid in my memory as if I still stood in front of her. The way her arms carved the air, flame coiling around her wrists, the hush of the crowd as she made a single spark blossom into a thousand petals of gold. How could such a beautiful thing be deemed forbidden? And if fire and its conjurers were truly of the devil…. Why did I find it so alluring?

"I know, Father," I muttered as my guilt threatened to strangle me. It was blasphemous to ask such questions, let alone want answers to them. "It is not for me." *She* was not for me.

"And yet you return to these spectacles."

Each time, I told myself it was the last. Each time... it wasn't. The sin of it was so familiar, it was almost a comfort.

"I'm sorry," I said, and I meant it, though not for the reasons Father Laurent probably wished. "I've prayed. I've tried. The urge doesn't go away."

His reply came softly, a gentle admonition. "Sin rarely does, Claude. It is the nature of temptation to persist. But you must persist also."

I nodded, my gesture lost in the darkness. He let the silence between us stretch, the air inside the box growing suffocating as the faint scent of smoke lingered in the air, likely from the candles burning nearby.

"I have seen the way you carry yourself," Father Laurent said at last. "You hold your head too high, using your rank as a shield. But it is a mask. A deflection. Pride is a sin, my child, even when it hides behind virtue."

My jaw tightened. I heard as much before in a dozen different ways: A woman should be meek, and a woman of my station even more so. My strength was a flaw, not a gift.

I wondered, sometimes, if another priest would have been kinder, more compassionate. But Paris had no shortage of men who found my devotion threatening, who believed God despised nothing more than a woman unwilling to kneel. If I could be remade in His likeness—pliant, penitent, grateful for the crumbs of dignity handed out by men—I would not have been sitting in this box, inhaling the growing cloud of smoke from Laurent's pipe.

"I will remember," I said as was expected, keeping my frustrations to myself. "Thank you, Father."

He issued the usual prescription: so many Hail Marys, a week of abstaining from wine, more time spent in solitary prayer. With a rustle of robes and a click of the latch, he dismissed me, the curtain fluttering shut to mark my return to the world of sin.

I lingered on the bench, waiting until Father Laurent's footsteps faded down the hall, and stepped out into the cathedral's cooling light. Tugging my sleeves straight, I squared my shoulders and made my way to the side altar, where the last of midday sun spilled through the stained glass windows, painting the floor with a rainbow. It was empty save for a few penitents hunched in the pews, their shadows trailing behind them. Accepting that now was as good a time as any to begin my penance, I knelt, allowing the wood to bite into my knees and clasping my hands together so tightly they ached.

More than anything, I wanted to pray, but the words wouldn't come. Not the rote ones—the ones I recited since childhood—and certainly not the secret, desperate pleas I used to whisper in the dark. *Fix me. Take away these sinful thoughts. Make me like everyone else. Please, God, I'll do anything.* It was pathetic, how much I loathed myself, but what lingered to this very day was worse. Daring to lift my head, I fixated on the martyrs lined along the walls, searching their painted, lifeless eyes for any spark of recognition.

Had they, too, ever found themselves fascinated with the thing they were supposed to fear?

Mages. It was a word spat with disgust from the instant I set foot in the Church as a child, a group I had been taught to despise above all others. They were people born with gifts allowing them to manipulate and command various elements, of which there were many: fire, water, and air were the most common, but there were ice mages, lightning mages, earth mages—even light and shadow mages. The Church said their powers were blasphemy, claiming their magic was sourced from demons of the worst sort. They were tricksters, illusionists, and couldn't be trusted.

Yet the more I was taught to hate them, the more impossible doing so became. The Church had targeted them for as long as anyone could remember, yet by all accounts, the mages were not only surviving, but thriving. They existed openly, refusing to retreat to the shadows, and I watched them whenever I could. At first from a distance, lurking in proximity of their gatherings, but never too close: the riverbank cabarets, the midnight duels, the markets they claimed solely for their kind. I convinced myself it was vigilance, a duty to bear witness to our enemy's tactics. Too soon, I recognized faces, anticipated their habits. Worst of all, I invented reasons to loiter in their vicinity. Not for spying… worse.

I, too, wished to so brazenly defy authority. To dress and speak and love who I pleased. To exist without apology.

And then—The Embermage. So help me God, I could never decide whether she was the worst or the best of them. As her name implied, she was a fire mage. A beloved dancer and an idol of the most sinful sort, given her gift to captivate the masses. Her immense power was undeniable, as was her presence while performing. I watched fire mages dance all my life, but never had another existed quite like her. She seemed made of flame herself, moving through her element as if it were water, her raven curls bouncing as she danced. I tried, once, to convince myself that it was the spectacle of her magic that drew me in, that seduced me so. But it wasn't her magic. It was *her*.

That first night, The Embermage wore a dark red skirt and sleeveless blouse, leaving her arms and shoulders bare, and her brown skin glimmered as if dusted in gold. She stepped onto the makeshift stage like a queen, the crowd pressing forward, every face upturned. She noticed none of them—not even me, standing at the edge of the torchlight, my Church robes marking me as a clear threat. But that was it: she wasn't there for us. She was there for herself, for her fire, for the impossible elegance of the element she conjured from nothing. A cloud of sparks, a ribbon of flame that curled around her wrist and vanished before it could burn her—if she *could* even be burned. I saw holy men handle relics with less reverence than she gave her own body.

Not as tall as me, but taller than I expected, The Embermage carried herself with the posture of a trained dancer and the smile of a woman who never lost anything she couldn't replace. Her hair was black as a raven's wing: its long, tight curls spilling over her back as she walked. Her eyes were emerald green, and when she looked at the crowd, she stared through them, as if she could use her flame to pluck out their every secret. I recalled the flick of her tongue over her lower lip when she concentrated, the sheen of sweat on her brow as she danced, the way she sometimes laughed at her own audacity, tossing her head back like it was nothing to be adored by a thousand strangers. I recalled, too, how I felt in those moments. Dizzy and free, as if she set something in me alight. I recalled, worst of all, how I returned to my room after, kneeling on the cold stone, begging for forgiveness I would never deserve.

What I could not confess to Father Laurent was that I didn't *want* forgiveness—not truly. I wanted to see her again, to stand in her crowd, invisible in my robes, and watch her conjure fire from nothing. I wanted to learn her secret, how she moved through the world without apology, how she held herself with such certainty. I wanted to touch her, to learn if her skin was as warm as it looked, if her hands would burn or bless.

But that was it. The desire itself was blasphemy of the same sort I'd been cursed with for as long as I could remember. The first time I ever craved another, it was a girl in convent school, with soft hands and a voice that recited psalms in perfect Latin, who pressed her lips to mine behind the pews when we were no more than children. We got caught, of course. She wept with terror, but I felt nothing but a cold, bracing clarity. The nuns called it demonic, a sickness of the mind, to be exorcised with prayer and fasting. But if it *was* a demon, it never left, not even when I outgrew my convent uniform and exchanged it for an Archdeacon's heavy velvet robes.

My sickness only deepened. To this day, I had frequent trysts with various partners—all of them women—which became frighteningly easy as I learned the art of discretion. By day, I kept my eyes down, voice level, my hands folded in the presence of temptation. But by night, several times a week, I indulged in sins of the flesh despite my vow of chastity. I learned about women: what they liked, how to pleasure them, and how to keep them coming back, if only to get my own indulgences met. I learned the world was filled with others like me—women who met and loved in secret, who found solace in the arms of the same sex despite the Church forbidding such acts.

Was The Embermage one of them?

The question rooted itself in my brain as the light flooding the cathedral grew richer. The sun slid further down the sky, casting a kaleidoscope of color across my still-clasped hands. My thoughts wandered, beyond the reach of Father Laurent and Notre Dame and any of the other prisons to which I was confined, and I imagined that somewhere across the city, The Embermage also watched as the day died.

I was still kneeling when the bells tolled again, this time six, and the hush of evening came over the cathedral. Not long after, footsteps scuffed behind me. I braced myself for the possibility of Laurent's return, but the footfalls were lighter, more erratic, followed by the unmistakable metallic clatter of something dropped and hastily retrieved. I recognized the rhythm, the uneven gait that echoed when he tried to move quietly. I turned without standing, and there stood my son, framed by the arch of the side aisle: Quasimodo, wearing his favorite purple shirt, his face so open in its hopefulness it summoned a smile to my own.

He lifted a hand, signing, *You're late.*

It was a running joke between us that I, whose existence orbited the tyranny of bells, could still lose track of time. I smiled wider, signing back, *Confession ran long.* A lie, but an innocent one.

Quasimodo grinned. He was fifteen now, nearing ever closer to adulthood, but when he smiled like that, it took me back to his boyhood years. Settling beside me, his fingers worked quickly and eagerly. *Faire, yes? We should leave soon.*

The anticipation in his gaze sliced me open. We attended the faire for the past six weeks straight, always on Friday evenings, always departing the cathedral around six. I didn't promise today would be the same, but I didn't say it wouldn't, either. No doubt Quasimodo could already taste the sugared almonds I always bought him, could picture the various performers who never failed to fascinate him… quite possibly including The Embermage. Last week, as I led us home in the darkness, I had no reason to believe I couldn't return one more time, if only to see my son smile. To believe that I could be, for one evening, a parent who gave their child the world, instead of my usual endless warnings of its dangers.

Now, after an hour of stewing in my wretchedness, and especially after Laurent's warnings, the prospect seemed impossible.

I shook my head, offering a small, apologetic smile. "Not tonight," I said, keeping my voice gentle, adding in sign, *Next week. I'm… not feeling well.*

Quasimodo's brow furrowed, disbelief and disappointment contorting his features in a way only teenagers could manage. *You promised.*

I know, I replied. *I'm sorry.* My hands moved with practiced grace, but my chest ached as I watched the hope leak out of him. I tried to soften the blow. *We can do something here if you like. Your choice.*

He looked away, jaw working, shoulders hunched, as if his disappointment held weight. For a long moment, he didn't sign or speak, just let the silence gnaw at us. *Why are you always tired, Maman? Are you sick?*

No answer would satisfy him, for I didn't have a good one. I couldn't tell him I was sick with self-loathing, with the gnawing ache of desire and the equally rabid fear of what would happen if I let it rule me. I couldn't tell him I was sick of lying, of trying to be what the Church wanted, of pretending to be a person who could be content within the oppressive stone of Notre Dame. I certainly couldn't tell him I was sick with longing for a woman who could never be mine.

"No, darling," I said aloud, then switched back to sign. *Not sick. Just… tired. The week has been draining.*

He arched an eyebrow. *Liar,* his hands said, blunt and irritated. I forced an awkward laugh, hoping to deflect, but he was relentless.

If you're not sick, why can't we go? He spelled each word with crisp precision, a clear sign of his anger.

Because I said so was the response that leapt to my lips. An old reflex, as automatic as breath. But I spent years trying not to become the kind of parent who weaponized their authority, who expected obedience for its own sake. I forced myself to be calm, to answer him as I would anyone else.

There are some things, I signed, barely managing to keep my fingers from quivering, *that I can't explain to you yet. Not because you're a child, but because they're difficult, even for me. I need you to trust me, Quasimodo.*

He scoffed. *Trust is earned.*

Despite being proof that I'd taught him well, the words stung more than I wanted to admit. I looked toward the flickering candles at the altar, the flames burning for someone's hope, someone's grief. I tried to remember what it felt like to pray when I still believed someone might be listening.

I turned back to him. *I know I've failed you. More than once. But I am trying—*

He cut me off, hands trembling as he signed, *You always say that. But nothing changes.*

"That isn't fair," I snapped aloud, surprised by the heat that crept to my cheeks. Though he couldn't hear my words or their echo, Quasimodo's mouth clamped shut. Silence hovered between us, thrumming with everything neither of us could say. I looked down at my hands and tried to peel back the anger, searching for what sorrow might be hiding underneath.

He shifted away from me, his face turned so I couldn't see the tremor in his jaw. "You're the only thing that changes," he said, and though his voice was soft, every syllable struck like a bell. "You never used to lie to me."

His truth undid me. I *had* taught him to value honesty above all else; promised him that whatever the world might take from us, we would always have truth. I became the very thing I swore to protect him from—a shield that was only ever a mask, just as Father Laurent had said.

I'm sorry, I signed, and this time I meant it so completely I could taste it, bitter as old communion wine. *It isn't fair to you. I know that.* I reached for him, but he jerked away, the movement so quick it nearly toppled him from the pew.

Quasimodo stood, huffing with indignation only a fifteen-year-old could summon. *I'm going to my room,* he signed, and strode off.

I stared after him. The cathedral was empty now, save for the flicker of votive candles and the faint, persistent clamor of the bells.

I could have gone after him, perhaps *should* have gone after him, but I knew from experience it would do no good. The boy was stubborn, and I'd given him every reason to be.

I pressed my palms together, knuckles white, and tried to summon some prayer that might reach him, or God, or anyone.

Nothing came.

After a while, I rose, knees numb, and limped to the archway leading to our private quarters. The stairs wound upward in a spiral, the stones worn smooth by centuries of feet. I paused at the landing before my son's door, listening to the muffled scrape of his chair as he settled in. I wanted to go in—to apologize, to promise something better—but the memory of Quasimodo's face, so tight with disappointment, stopped me cold.

I retreated instead to my room, the one overlooking the river, leaving my door open a crack just in case. For a while, I stood at the window, letting the breeze wash over my face. The city glimmered, dusk settling over the rooftops like a blanket on a restless child. The Seine ferried its secrets downstream, the water reflecting the last golden tongues of sunlight. In the distance, a plume of smoke curled lazily, rising above the square where the night markets stirred to life. The Embermage would be there, preparing for her performance, dressing in elaborate costume and dusting her cheeks with gold. I envied her ability to become someone else so completely, if only for a night.

Turning away, I paced the length of my chamber, the floor as cold as my regret. I had never been one for decoration, but tonight, my room seemed especially barren; perhaps that was yet another reason

I so often invited women here. My desk, my battered trunk, and my simple bed—its blankets pressed and untouched since morning after I threw out my partner and hastily changed the sheets—were the room's only occupants. The fireplace was unlit, but the scent of old ash lingered. Above it on the mantle sat Quasimodo's latest wood carving: a miniature Notre Dame, each spire askew. He pressed it into my palm last week, his face expectant, and I tried not to weep at the way he still sought my approval despite the ever-widening rift between us.

Crossing back to the window, I pressed my forehead against the thick glass, watching the streetlamps flicker to life. My reflection was a ghostly double, pale and severe, eyes rimmed with exhaustion I could never seem to shake. Other than my short hair, I looked like my mère, or at least how I imagined she must have looked before her untimely death. My unusual hair color, a silvery white, was from her, but I neither knew nor remembered much else about her. I wondered, as I often did, whether she ever stood in a room such as this, weighed down by similar burdens and the same impossible desires.

The sound of Quasimodo's door closing one floor down was my cue to give up the idea of reconciliation, at least for tonight. I shut my own, turned the lock, and swept the heavy curtain across the threshold for extra measure. A chill pressed in, so I knelt at the hearth and struck flint to tinder, coaxing a hesitant flame from the brittle sticks. It caught, then grew stronger, the flame's orange tongue flickering at the logs. I watched it for a long time, waiting for the heat to drive away the cathedral's chill, waiting for my mind to quiet. It didn't.

So I stood, unfastening my collar and loosening the stiff velvet of my vestments. Piece by piece, I shed the day's armor: the outer robe, the heavy surplice, the long linen undershirt that clung to my flattened chest. Alone, I allowed myself the small, illicit comfort of standing in only the borrowed silhouette I chose. Plain black trousers, a white shirt, sleeves rolled to the elbow. The fire grew, painting shadows against the stone. The tension in my body began to release, as if I were exhaling for the first time since morning.

Affirming as it was, I couldn't dwell in a fantasy forever. My reluctant fingers, clumsy with exhaustion, worked at the final buttons of the shirt. The linen was damp where I sweated through, ringed with salt at the pits and collar. I peeled it away, shivering as air touched my bare skin. In the faint glow of the hearth, I looked at my chest. A latticework of bandages, wound tight and flat, was the only way I could bear to be seen. The first time I bound myself, I was no more than twelve, desperate to erase the curve of my growing body. I had nearly fainted from the pain, but that agony was a mercy compared to the alternative. Years later, the binding remained a ritual, an act of faith as much as penance, and I performed it with the same reverence as I did the Eucharist. Undoing them was always the hardest part. I waited until the room was fully dark, save for the pulsing glow of fire, before beginning. Slow and deliberate, I let each unwrapping bring me closer to the shape I despised.

When the last strip came away, I balled it in my fist and sat cross-legged on the floor, staring blankly into the flames. The heat was a balm, but my mind was merciless. I mourned the body I'd been given, marking me an impostor in my own life. I mourned the way my voice, my hands, my stride in the corridors—all things I worked so hard to perfect—could be undone by a glance, a slip, a single word from someone who saw too much. I wished, in that moment, to vanish entirely, to burn away all that was false and emerge as something new, something worthy of the hunger that gnawed at my insides.

Smoke curled from the hearth, thick and persistent. I had piled the kindling too high. The air grew hazy, the flames shifting and reshaping themselves with a hypnotic grace. The fire bent and bowed, flickering in a dance that was at once foreign and familiar. In the wavering shadows, I saw The Embermage—her arms raised, her silhouette limned in gold, her eyes bright as molten glass. I imagined her circling the fire, the hem of her skirt catching the light, each step measured and deliberate. I pictured her stopping before me, close enough to feel the heat radiating from her skin, her breath sweet with smoke.

The fantasy took on a life of its own. I watched her dance, watched as flames wrapped around her wrists and throat, watched as she stepped through the fire and came to kneel beside me, her hands gentle as she reached for my face.

The Embermage cupped my cheek with one hand, thumb tracing the ridge of my jaw before moving to the nape of my neck—and I let her. She smelled of lilac and woodsmoke, yet something sweeter and more forbidden still. Her lips parted as she pressed closer, knees touching mine, searching my face for permission. Despite never kissing anyone on the lips since that convent girl, I nodded. She leaned in, her cheek brushing mine with a softness that undid me completely. The heat of her mouth, the passion of her tongue, and the weight of her body settled against my own. There was no audience here, no Church, no Laurent, no crowd. Only us.

In the waking world, my hands were restless. I pressed my palm against my chest, above my heart, feeling the wildness of its beat. The other drifted lower, finding my waistband—vows shattering, as they always did, under the weight of need.

I let myself imagine it, fully, recklessly, as I hadn't dared in months. The Embermage's lips trailed down my throat, her hands slipped beneath my shirt, and her fingers drew patterns of heat over every inch of bare skin. In the fantasy, she undid me with a laugh, with a look, with the promise of a thousand forbidden things. Her breath was on my ear, teeth grazing my flesh, her voice an alluring whisper: "You're allowed, you know. To want."

I wanted her. God help me, I wanted her so much it hurt.

Before I thought of stopping myself, I pressed my palm between my legs and let my head fall back, eyes closing against the orange pulse of the fire. I pictured The Embermage standing above me, all shadow and light, the sweep of her arms summoning flame and snuffing it out. I imagined her hands undoing my bindings, not with gentleness, but with impatience, with the same hunger I witnessed in her performances. I imagined her voice, low and urgent: "Let me see you. *All* of you."

The words were a benediction, a commandment more sacred than any I received at the altar. I obeyed without hesitation. My hips bucked upward, the ache in my core only worsening. The imagined hands of The Embermage slipped beneath my own, guiding, coaxing, worshiping. I gasped, the sound half-swallowed by the hush of the room, my fingers tightening on the tender flesh of my thigh. I wanted to cry out, to beg, to confess everything I had ever felt, but the only sound that escaped me was a thin, desperate whimper.

In the flickering light, the smoke thickened, curling around my bare shoulders like a lover's embrace. The fire's heat pressed against my skin, every nerve ending alive with want. I rocked against my palm, the rhythm urgent, the pressure building until it was too much to bear. I pictured her mouth closing over my breast, her tongue flickering hot and wet, her teeth scraping just enough to make me shudder. I imagined her hands pushing me down, holding me there, her gaze never leaving mine.

When I came, it was with a violence that shocked me. Heat rippled through me with shattering force, leaving me breathless and trembling, clutching myself as if afraid I might come apart. I bit my knuckle hard enough to draw blood, stifling a cry that would have otherwise echoed throughout the cathedral—a damning betrayal I couldn't afford. As the orgasm's tremors at last began to cease, it occurred to me the air was so thick with smoke I could barely see, my eyes streaming with tears, my skin tingling. A dark, involuntary chuckle escaped me. Instead of sending angels, God had once again allowed a demon in my presence.

Fine. I sat up just enough to assume the familiar position of penance. *I will atone, Father.*

It was impossible to say how long I knelt there, head bowed, tasting the ash of my sin.

II. THE COMMUNITY

Esmeralda

There were far too many guards here.

If my mère taught me anything, it was never to give our so-called 'protectors' more than a second glance, much less a thought. But even she would have been unnerved by their increased presence in the mages' market—*our* sanctuary, *our* domain. Around every corner, there stood another, bored and visibly irritated to observe a crowd they had been taught to regard as vermin. It was a small comfort to note they were young, new to the city, and profoundly uninterested in our affairs, especially those as mundane as our market. I counted three with their arms crossed, whose fingers tapped against their sides in a rhythm that betrayed their impatience. Still, their presence unsettled the market's usual energy. The vendors' calls came softer, the laughter more cautious, the children darting between stalls with eyes wide and wary.

I refused to let it ruin my morning.

If my plan was to have any hope of playing out the way I envisioned, I needed to appear untroubled and confident. Weaving through the crowd, I kept my posture loose, my chin high, and my smile wide. The late afternoon air was cold and bright, sunlight slicing through the tangle of colored awnings and catching on hanging beads, glass vials, and the metallic shimmer of enchanted jewelry. The market was a riot of color, alive with the scent of cinnamon and sugared almonds. Even with the guards prowling and the recent tension with the Church etched onto every face, the air buzzed with stubborn joy. That was our way: when the world made itself hostile, when it treated our magic as something to be feared rather than celebrated, we clung to our hope and snatched it wherever we could.

As I continued wandering, I noted my sibling, Jules, was nowhere in sight. I expected as much. Preferring to leave the mundane tasks of running our household to me, Jules's mornings were more often spent curled around Antoine, who worked nights at the infirmary, and neither could be roused before noon unless the building was on fire—a scenario that, in fairness, occurred more than once. Another day, their absence may have irked me, but today, it meant I was unaccompanied. I relished the freedom, especially after a night spent performing, catering to an entire crowd's desires. That said, the last thing I needed was my sibling asking questions.

I had a mission to accomplish—one I didn't need them meddling in.

Rounding the final corner, I kept said mission in mind as I reached the square's heart. The booths here had always been my favorite, perhaps because their vendors reminded me of my mére: loud, opinionated, and impossible to ignore. At the apothecary's table, a pair of older women argued over the correct ratio for foxglove elixir, conducting business with a line of customers who reveled in their bickering. They recognized me, as everyone in the quarter did, but not as The Embermage. Here, I was Esmeralda Derosiers, daughter of Clopin and Carmen, sister to Jules, descended from some of the most gifted fire mages our kind had ever known. The alias was necessary only for those outside the mage community, a shield that had the added benefit of adding to my stage allure. As I passed, one of the apothecary owners winked, passing me a candied violet without breaking the rhythm of her squabble. I popped it into my mouth, savoring the sharp sweetness and the way it lingered, bright and defiant against the chill in the air.

Beyond them, a cluster of young mages sat huddled around a chessboard made of ice, its pieces frosted and glimmering. One of them, an earth mage with a tangle of brown curls, flashed a grin, his fingers gathering a pebble from the ground to offer as a bet. I shook my head, grinning back, and drifted on.

Everywhere I looked, there was evidence of our resilience. At the far end of the row, the elderly earth mage who sold me my first flameproof gloves as a child coaxed a patch of out-of-season violets to bloom from a crack in the flagstones. A lightning mage's apprentice, no older than twelve, sparred with her mentor using the market's metal fixtures as a conductor, their laughter a high, wild cackle that sent the nearby guards wincing. By the well, a water mage demonstrated his talent for purifying the cistern, drawing a crowd of onlookers who clapped when he finished. None of it was strictly legal, but here, within the bounds of our own, it was as natural as breathing. That was what the Church would never understand: our magic wasn't spectacle, pride, or even rebellion. It was survival.

I ducked beneath a string of bright paper lanterns, remembering the first time I came to this market. Maman's hand had been warm and strong in my own, her voice low as she whispered the names of each flower, face, and curse traded above the heads of the guards. She knew every vendor, every secret passage through the alleys, every trick to extract an extra sweet from the confectioner. I could have sworn she was beside me once more as she laughed, a sound that made strangers turn and smile without knowing why. I savored it, though it was just a trick of memory.

A sudden splash of cold startled me from my thoughts. I was caught in the wake of a small child running from an older sibling, both soaked to the knees and shrieking with delight as they weaved through the crowd. The younger one's hair sparked with static— lightning magic in early bloom—and when he saw me watching, he stuck out his tongue. I couldn't help but laugh, the sound carrying further than I intended. So far, it drew the attention of a nearby guard, who turned with wary suspicion. Unflinching, I met his gaze, daring him to do more than glare. When he finally looked away, I lifted my chin and moved on, heart hammering with the familiar mixture of defiance and adrenaline.

I would not—*could* not—let them see me weak.

I made my way to the square's farthest edge, where the oldest of the market's vendors set up shop. The air here was steeped with the scent of parchment and damp wool, and there were far fewer bodies to navigate. This left more room for secrets to pass between those who knew how to listen. I paused at a tiny, crooked stall draped in a patchwork of faded silks, its shelves stacked with glass bottles in every imaginable color. Behind the counter, a woman with silver-threaded braids and sharp, severe features looked up from her ledger.

"Esmeralda," she said, her voice as rough as gravel but warm with maternal fondness. "You're late."

"I'm never late, Tante Mirielle," I replied, grinning. "You just like to pretend as much so you can scold me."

She snorted, tucking a strand of hair behind her ear. "Perhaps." Reaching beneath the counter, she produced a wrapped parcel, the brown paper sealed with a splash of red wax. "Tell Jules not to consume it all at once, or I'll make the next batch taste like vinegar."

"Jules isn't the only one who takes these," I reminded her, lowering my voice, "and I've got *plans* for this week's performance."

Tante Mirielle grunted, waving her hand dismissively. "Hush, child. You know a performer ought not to reveal all her secrets."

I tucked the package into my satchel, feeling its gentle warmth through the fabric—a telltale sign of the fireproofing potion inside. Tante Mirielle's potions were the best in the quarter, dangerous enough to be contraband but subtle enough to pass as perfume if one knew how to be careful. I handed her the coins, which she pocketed without looking, never breaking the rhythm of her survey of the market.

"Quiet day," I said, gesturing to the relative emptiness.

She shrugged. "The Church is everywhere, and people are afraid. But not you. You're strutting around like you own the place."

"Don't I?"

Tante Mirielle's gaze softened as she snorted, her eyes darting over my face with the easy affection of family not bound by blood. "Not yet. But you're getting there, *petite braise*."

It was a compliment, a warning, and a prayer all wrapped into one. I took it as intended and prepared to move on. But Tante Mirielle's hand shot out, catching my wrist before I could step away.

"Careful," she said, her voice pitched low enough to vanish beneath the market's drone. "There's talk of a raid tonight. The new Captain of the Guard's been asking after you, specifically."

"Let him ask," I replied, shrugging. What was that bastard's name again—Phineas, Phoenix? "I don't answer to the Church, and I have nothing to hide."

She squeezed my wrist, then let go. "That's what Carmen said. Right before—"

I looked away, suddenly more fascinated by the arrangement of colored glass on her table than I was at the mention of Maman's name. "I know."

A silence settled, heavy as it was awkward.

"If you see Jules, tell them I need two more sets of ledgers," Tante Mirielle said, returning to business. "And you—don't do anything stupid."

I grinned, my mask snapping back into place. "Tante Mirielle, have you met me?"

Her laughter was as sharp as broken glass. "That's why I keep a fire-extinguishing potion behind the counter. Now get out of here before I find more chores for you."

I left before she could; her warnings rather than her jokes echoed in my ears.

The market's far end opened onto a quieter lane, where the crowd thinned to a trickle. I lingered in the shadow of an awning, savoring the momentary peace, and let myself think—*really* think— about the plan I had obsessed over for days. My planned seduction of the silver-haired man, the one clearly from the Church who haunted every one of my performances since midsummer, was a scheme so audacious it was almost laughable. He was impossible to miss, hovering at the edge of the faire, always in the same reserved stance: arms folded, face covered by the hood of his cloak, and a look of wary curiosity that said he was both fascinated and terrified by what he saw. I recognized the hunger in his gaze on the first night, and it delighted me to know I had that effect even on the most pious of people.

But he didn't come last night. That was unusual.

I told myself it meant nothing. He probably had a lover or some other secret to keep—the boy who accompanied him could very well be his son, but that didn't mean the Church viewed the child as legitimate. Perhaps they ordered them never to return. Maybe the silver-haired man's obvious curiosity for me had burned out, or worse, shifted elsewhere. I should have been relieved, but the hollow ache of disappointment was so keen I could have sworn it belonged to someone else, or to a younger, more foolish version of myself. The plan, though, was not about him. It was about us: the mages, the market, the lives that would be snuffed out if we allowed the Church to dictate how we were seen and heard.

It was the sole reason I came here today. I needed something—*anything*—to lure the silver-haired man back to my shows. A prop, a costume… Hell, I'd prance about the stage naked if that's what it took to see him return. But it couldn't be too obvious, either. I knew the harder I pushed, the more likely he was to run.

I needed to ensnare him completely, and the potion from Tante Mirielle would help me do it.

Drawing my jacket tighter, the cold sliced sharper now that I was alone. The avenue here was lined with leafless plane trees, and the breeze carried a tang of woodsmoke and roasting chestnuts from the next street over. I pictured how I might stage my next performance: how I might lure the silver-haired man back to the edge of the crowd, how I might give him a show so beautiful and dangerous he'd forget his vows, his Church, his very self. I would make it seductive, wrap a ribbon of flame around my waist, call him onto the stage and dare him to touch it. To touch *me*. The idea filled me with a dangerous sort of delight. I didn't want to humiliate him—I wanted him to want me, to collapse the space between us, to let everyone see one of the Church's most precious yearning for an outcast like me.

"Daydreaming again, Esme?" The voice was low, sly, and unmistakably familiar: Henrietta, whose stall specialized in textiles and gossip. She sat perched on a crate, knitting with needles that glowed at the tips, their yarn a shifting, iridescent blue.

"Henri, if you ever learn to keep your nose in your own business, I'll eat my hat," I shot back, sidling up to her table. She offered a lopsided grin and flicked her needles, the yarn twisting itself into a perfect double knot.

"I'd pay to see that," she said, eyes flicking up and down my coat. "But I'd have to make you one first." Her gaze sharpened, and she gestured with her chin toward the far end of the lane. "You see them?"

I followed her gaze. A pair of guards, leaning against a lamppost. One had a fresh black eye while the other nursed a hand bandaged in white, the cloth already spotted with blood. Both looked like they'd rather be anywhere but here.

"Thought they'd get bored by now," I said. "Or at least learn to be less obvious."

"They're not here for us," Henrietta replied, lowering her voice. "Not directly. You know the Sirot family, over on Rue des Martyrs?"

I did. The Sirots were earth mages, quiet and respectable, their only so-called crime being the cultivation of a rooftop vegetable garden that fed half their block—but that was it, wasn't it? "They came for them?" I asked as the realization struck, my whisper incredulous.

Henrietta nodded, her lips pressed into a thin line. "Dragged the parents out before sunrise. No warrant, no charge. Just gone."

I felt something inside me twist and snap, the emotion so raw my flames threatened to ignite. "What about the kids?"

"They're gone, too."

I let the information settle, cold and heavy. This was how it started: one family, one arrest, and the rest of us left to wonder if we'd be next. The Sirots were harmless, which was exactly why the Church came for them. The ones who kept their heads down, who didn't dare to make a fuss, who thought they could pass through the world without attracting notice—they were the first to fall. All my life, I'd been told to watch the quiet ones. I just never thought I'd have to mourn them, too.

"I'll talk to Papa, the Council." My mind continued to race as words tumbled out, hoarse and panicked. "They won't let this stand, they won't just sit back like cow—"

"Clopin already announced they're doing all they can, and cooperating with Church authorities," Henrietta cut across me, her voice gentle. "Which likely means they're doing nothing."

No. I nearly snapped, but I bit my tongue. As much as I didn't want to admit it, ever since they'd taken my mère, Papa had kept his head down as much as he could, not wanting his fellow Council members to lose their spouses or children, or for the Church to retaliate more violently than they already had. *It's about protecting the community,* he'd assured me over and over again. So why did my community feel like the farthest thing from protected right now?

Henrietta leaned closer, her words little more than a whisper on the wind as she echoed my thoughts. "If they can take the Sirots, they can take any of us. Doesn't matter how careful you are."

I nodded, my jaw set so tight it hurt. I pressed my hand against the front of my jacket, feeling for the necklace beneath. The ruby pendant hidden in my clothes had been my mère's, the only thing of hers I managed to keep after the night they came for us. The memory was a knife: the way her hand curled around mine, the press of her lips to my forehead, the last, wild spark in her eyes as she turned to face the guards. She'd always said they could take anything from her—her freedom, her pride, her life—but they would never take her magic. *Never let them see you afraid, Es*, she whispered in the dark. *Never let them think they've won.*

I'd worn her pendant every day since, the stone growing warm against my skin whenever I thought of her.

Henrietta's gaze softened when she caught the gesture. "Carmen would be proud," she said so quietly I almost didn't hear.

I shrugged it off, unwilling to let Henrietta see how much hearing Maman's name, twice in one day now, affected me. "She'd be furious I let you corner me this long. I have errands." It was all I could do not to blurt out the nature of said 'errands'—it was impossible to say whether Henrietta would be horrified, impressed, or both if she knew of my intention to seduce the silver-haired man.

"Wait." Henrietta flicked her needles again, and the blue scarf she'd been working on folded itself into her lap. "Have you heard the rumors about what's under the Palais Garnier?"

I rolled my eyes. I didn't have time for this nonsense, and if anyone other than Henrietta tried to spew it to me, I'd have walked away. "Unless you're about to tell me the Sirots are hiding there, I'm not interested."

"Not them. *Him.*"

I groaned. "The old ghost stories? The tunnels, the masked man, all that?"

Henrietta grinned, her teeth sharp and white against her brown skin. "It's not just stories, Esme. My cousin's apprentice met a man who says he lives down there, who walks through the catacombs as if he knows them from memory. Some kind of air mage, but not like any we've seen. They say he's got a mask that covers half his face, and he can walk through walls if he wants to."

I snorted. "He can walk through walls, but chooses to haunt an opera house? Sounds like a waste of magic if I've ever heard one."

Henrietta's brows lifted. "He's got a whole enclave down there. A safe house. For the ones who can't show their faces in the market anymore." She leaned in, voice dropping further. "They say he's building something. Some kind of army. Or maybe a revolution. I figured you'd want to know, especially if you plan to go after the Sirots. For all we know, maybe they *are* down there."

Henrietta always managed to make her wildest gossip sound like prophecy. But I grew up on stories of secret societies and shadow rebels, and I didn't have the luxury of believing in ghosts when there were plenty of real monsters above ground. "I'm not going after them." *Not yet, anyway.* "And if I ever get desperate enough to hide in a haunted opera house, I'll let you know. Until then, tell your cousin's apprentice to lay off the absinthe."

She laughed and flicked her needles, already deep in her next row. "Suit yourself. But you're missing out. The masked man's supposed to be quite the romantic."

"Not my type," I called over my shoulder, and let the hum of the market swallow me up.

I lost myself in the steady thrum of the crowd, letting the conversation with Henrietta fade into the background noise of the city. My thoughts lingered only a moment on the image of a masked man pacing the gilded corridors of the Palais Garnier before fixating instead on the silver-haired man. It was curious how he'd so thoroughly consumed my thoughts these past weeks—not solely because he was of the Church, but because he was a man. I bedded them before, but it was as I told Henrietta, they didn't tend to be my type. A person's appearance or gender didn't matter as much to me as their hearts, their souls. Still, it couldn't be denied that I had a strong preference for women, or at least feminine-presenting people, and there were plenty in the mage community.

Maybe that was why the silver-haired man lingered in my memory with such persistence. He was an anomaly, a disruption to every pattern I constructed around my desires. His presence at my performances, always standing in the same spot, always with his son in tow, was a riddle I returned to compulsively. I wanted to believe my fixation was strategy. What better way to distract a man of the Church than with a spectacle so overwhelming it eclipsed his sense of duty? But I couldn't deny the way he made my pulse jump, the way I sometimes felt him watching even when I was backstage, out of sight.

He haunted me as no one else ever had.

As I drifted back into the market's current, my attention caught on Henrietta's scarf. The color, that luminous blue, shimmered in the late sun like a fragment of sky. With that image in mind, I found myself drawn to the fabric merchants, their stalls crowded with bolts of silk, velvet, and wool in every color and pattern. I'd never cared much for fashion beyond what was necessary for the stage—my costumes were armor, nothing more—but the idea of a new prop, something to sharpen the edge of my next performance, took root in my mind.

Have I found my weapon at last?

I let my hands wander the displays, trailing over soft folds of velvet, the crisp edge of linen, the impossible slipperiness of raw silk. None of it felt right until the very last stall, where a weaver I barely recognized fussed over a loom. She was new, or at least relatively new, with a mass of pale hair pinned in a messy knot and a way of never making direct eye contact. Her sign, hand-painted and warped at the corners, read: "*For Those Who Dress To Be Remembered.*" It was, I had to admit, an excellent slogan.

The fabric draped over the front of her booth was unlike anything I'd ever seen. It was a scarf, but calling it that was an insult; it was more like a veil, or a ribbon, or some combination of the two. It was almost completely sheer, but its colors—violet, with undertones of midnight blue—shifted with the light so that as I moved, it seemed to move with me, as if it were alive. The edges were weighted with the tiniest glass beads, each one a different shade of amethyst, so that the entire piece shimmered like starlight.

I reached out, half-expecting the weaver to snap at me. Instead, she gave me a small, nervous smile, her hands never pausing in their work. "You can touch it," she said, voice soft and scratchy. "It won't bite."

I ran my fingers over the scarf's length. It was as light as smoke, cooler than silk, and softer than anything I'd ever worn. "It's beautiful," I said, unable to keep the awe from my voice.

The weaver ducked her head, flustered. "It's enchanted to catch the light, and remembers the last person who wore it. Not their face, but the shape of their longing. It's perfect for performers." She looked up, her gaze sharp and assessing. "It would suit you."

I didn't bother to haggle; the scarf was exactly what I needed, and I knew already I'd find no other like it. "I'll take it," I said, and when she named her price—steep, but not outrageous—I paid it in full, tucking the delicate cloth into my satchel.

As I walked away, I imagined how I'd use it. The next time the silver-haired man appeared at my show, I'd single him out and draw him up from the crowd with a mere gesture. I'd let the scarf unfurl in the torchlight, let it snake around my wrist, then slip from my fingers, a violet ribbon stretching across the gap between us. He'd reach for it, hesitating, but unable to help himself. When the scarf wound around his hand, I'd pull him forward—slowly, a moth drawn to the flame. I'd let the fabric slide over his knuckles, then up his arm, until it circled the back of his neck. Only then would I close the distance, lips so close to his ear he could feel the heat of my breath, but not the touch of my lips. I'd leave him trembling and ruined, the longing on his face a wound visible to everyone.

If I were feeling truly cruel, I'd let the scarf linger on his shoulder as he returned to the crowd. I smiled to myself, already anticipating the play of light and shadow, the way the crowd would hush, all eyes on the two of us.

Lost in my visions, I barely noticed the shift in my surroundings. The sun dipped lower, the air turning brittle and sharp. The market was empty now, the vendors packing up their wares in a hurry, eyes darting to corners where the guards gathered in clusters, their faces more stern than ever. I took that as my cue to leave, winding through the back lanes and up the long set of stairs that led to our house.

We lived in one of the old limestone manses on Rue des Templiers, a fact that still felt vaguely absurd to me. Papa's position on the Mage's Council afforded us a degree of comfort bordering on luxury, but after well over a decade, I never quite shook the feeling that we were guests in a world keen to evict us the moment we became inconvenient. The house itself was a sprawling, drafty thing, its every surface lined with books, dried herbs, and the occasional relic my père had "liberated" from the Church's archives. The only room untouched by clutter was the kitchen, which Jules ruled with an iron fist and a collection of knives so sharp they could split a hair.

I let myself in, resisting the urge to slam the door and announce my presence. It was pointless. Jules had an uncanny sense for my movements, and by the time I hung my coat and kicked off my boots, they were already there, perched on the edge of the kitchen counter. They peeled a blood orange with efficiency usually reserved for surgery. Segments accumulated in a perfect spiral on the cutting board, the rind discarded with disdain. When Jules cut, the world faded to white noise, and I watched them work, dropping my guard a bit now that every breath I took wasn't being scrutinized by city guards.

Jules didn't look up. "You're late," they said, echoing Tante Mirielle.

"Wasn't aware you'd be waiting up for me," I replied, dropping my satchel with a clatter onto the bench.

"'Course I waited. I've been bored for hours." Jules flicked a segment of blood orange into their mouth, chewed, and deigned to turn their sharp hazel eyes on me. "You get what you needed?"

I shrugged, making a show of fishing through the satchel as if it were a bottomless pit of secrets. "Enough for a small army, or one very dramatic exit," I said, waving the parcel from Tante Mirielle.

Jules grunted, unimpressed. "We still have half a bottle left from last week, you know."

"That batch is barely enough to do my hair, let alone light the whole stage."

They nearly choked on their orange. "You're not lighting the *whole stage*...are you? You told Henrietta the last show would be 'low-key,' then did the finale with your sleeves on fire."

"People like a little drama," I said, feigning innocence. "It's not my fault if the audience prefers a spectacle."

Jules's gaze was sharp enough to cut. "You're going to get yourself killed one of these days. Or worse, exiled."

I snorted. "Since when were you the careful one?"

They popped another segment into their mouth, ignoring me. "Papa's already worried. He says the Council's under more scrutiny than ever, what with the Sirots' disappearance."

Gossip travelled faster than Henrietta could spew it if Jules had already heard about the Sirots. But Papa was always worried, and the Council had been under 'more scrutiny' since the year I was born. I didn't say as much aloud; there was an unspoken rule between me and Jules that we didn't discuss such things in the house, our sanctuary. Instead, I cleared a spot at the table and flopped into a chair, the fatigue of the day finally catching up to me. Jules remained perched on the counter, legs swinging, waving a small knife between their fingers. They looked at me, unblinking, and despite the heavy topic we'd glossed over, I sensed the interrogation wasn't over.

"So?" Jules said. "What's the scarf for?"

I tried to adopt a look of bland surprise, but the look wasn't lost on my sibling, whom I hadn't been able to lie to since they were five. Still, it was worth a try. "Scarf? What scarf?"

Jules's eyes narrowed, the knife stopping mid-spin. "The one you're trying not to stare at every three seconds." They hopped off the counter, crossed the kitchen, and in one fluid motion, plucked the scarf from my satchel. "This thing?" They held it up, letting the violet fabric unfurl and catch the light. It shimmered between us, a living thing, and Jules's expression shifted from one of suspicion to something close to awe.

"Careful," I said, reaching for it, but Jules was faster, skipping backward and looping the scarf around their neck with a theatrical flourish.

"This is more than a prop," they said, voice mischievous. "Is it for a new routine, or are you planning to strangle someone in their sleep?"

"Neither," I said, lunging again, but they dodged me, winding the scarf tighter around their throat, letting the beads clink together in a faint, musical way.

"Is this part of your obsession with that Church man?" Jules's lip curled, half disgust, half intrigue.

"That's none of your fucking business."

"It is if you plan to bring that *filth* into our house."

I shot back my retort without missing a beat, though I hated how desperate I sounded. "You don't know anything about him, and I never said anything about bringing him here."

Jules flung the scarf over their shoulder and crossed their arms. "I know more than enough to stay away, and you should too. He's clergy, Es. He's not here for you—he's here to see what you'll do, and then he'll run to his masters with your name in his mouth."

"That's not true."

Jules barked a laugh. "You think you're the first to fall for a Church man looking sad and pathetic? To think you can fix that void in their souls they're always scrambling to fill??" They shook their head, the pale ends of the scarf fanning like a flag of surrender.

"At least be honest about what you want."

I had to grip the edge of the table to keep my hands still, but more importantly, to prevent flames from erupting through my skin. "You don't know what I want," I said, my voice low and threatening. "You don't know anything—"

"Don't I?" Jules's eyes glinted. "You want him to break. You want him to crawl, to beg, to burn for you so badly he'd give up his God." Each word sliced ever deeper. "You want him to belong to you because you've never belonged to anyone. Not really."

I dove for the scarf, letting fire spark in my hands just enough to singe the air. Jules grinned, delighted by my loss of composure, and held the scarf up, out of reach, their body angled between me and the prize.

"Give it back," I snarled. "You'll ruin it."

"What's the real plan, Es?" Jules kept their composure as well as their lightning at bay, while I continued clawing at them. "You think you can change him? Or are you hoping he'll change you?"

I hated that question. Hated it so much I nearly let my hands erupt, right then and there in the kitchen, but the memory of Maman's voice—*never let them see you afraid*—held me back. I forced myself to breathe, to remember all the ways Jules got under my skin in the past and how, every time, it was because they cared too much, not too little.

"Neither," I said too sharply. So sharp, the words came out like a curse. "I just want him to admit he wants me. That's it. I want him to say it out loud. Is that so monstrous?"

Jules's grin faltered, replaced by something more brittle. "You want him to suffer."

"Maybe I do," I said, voice rising. "Maybe I want someone else to be the fool for once. Maybe I'm tired of pretending it doesn't hurt, tired of wanting things I can't have. Maybe—"

A surge of water erupted between us with the force of a slap, cold and sudden as a storm. It drenched the table, the scarf, and both our faces, hissing as it hit the sparks in my hands and sending a fine mist scattering through the air. Jules and I blinked in unison, sputtering, as the water rolled off us and pooled on the tiled floor.

Antoine stood in the archway, arms crossed, hair still damp from his shower, and a look of resigned exasperation on his face. "You two are going to burn down the house again," he said, not bothering to raise his voice.

Jules's cheeks went bright red, and they scowled, but the effect was ruined by the way their curls stuck to their forehead. For a second, the three of us stood in awkward silence: me, dripping and furious; Jules, clutching the scarf like a lifeline; and Antoine, calm and collected.

He strode across the kitchen, stepping over the puddle as if it were nothing, and plucked the scarf from Jules's neck. "You're both idiots," he said, shaking his head, but the look he gave Jules was one of fondness, without a hint of malice. To me, he offered a towel. I took it, blinking away the sting left by Jules's words.

"You two finish this later," Antoine said, "or I'll make you both help me at work tomorrow. And Es, if you're going to spar, do it outside. The neighbors already complain about the noise."

He handed the scarf back to me. I clutched it tight, the beads clicking against each other as my hands shook.

Jules shot me a look, equal parts apology and challenge, then slid off the counter and stalked out, Antoine following with a hand resting on the small of their back.

The kitchen fell silent, save for the faint drip of water off the table's edge. I sat motionless, the towel pressed to my face, waiting for my pulse to slow. The fight with Jules left me gutted, but it was the truth in their accusation that lingered, sharp as a splinter: *You want him to burn for you.*

When I could finally breathe without wanting to set the room on fire, I stood, wrung out the scarf, and tiptoed up the stairs to my room. The door creaked open to reveal the same chaos I left behind that morning: books stacked three and four deep along every available shelf, a tangle of costumes draped over the foot of my bed, and a mirror propped against the wall, its surface clouded by last night's stage makeup. I shut the door behind me, pressing my back to it, and exhaled.

Walking to the mirror, the image it contained wasn't my own. The Embermage stared back: the confident performer, the seductress who commanded a crowd's adoration with a single glance. Beneath that, though, was the flicker of doubt Jules ignited. Was this, too, just a role I slipped into? A persona, worn like a second skin?

My gaze drifted from the reflection to the space beside it. I pictured the silver-haired man there, not in his Church robes, but naked. I imagined him next to me, his composure fractured, his face flushed with a desire he'd been taught to name as sin.

The fantasy took root, vicious and sharp, revealing a provocative truth: it wasn't enough for him to want me in the dark. I wanted him to *see* me, to kneel beside me, forced to meet his tormented reflection in the glass. To bear witness to his surrender, to watch the mask of his piety crumble and fall away, leaving only the raw, desperate hunger that simmered beneath. He would watch himself come undone at my hands, a beautiful, private martyrdom for an audience of one. *Me.*

A shiver of power coursed through my veins, not simply igniting my flames, but feeding them. This was no longer a vague, hastily thrown-together plan. It was a scene, a performance where I was the choreographer of his downfall. This fixation, this lust I felt—it wasn't weakness. It was my script.

I smirked at my reflection, a slow, dangerous curve of the lips. My determination renewed, colder and sharper than before. The Church called it corruption.

I called it justice.

III. THE PENANCE

Claude

I blinked, and it was Friday once more.

The week passed in a haze. I remembered fragments: the ragged edge of Quasimodo's disappointment, the never-ending penance assigned by Father Laurent, the mindless repetition of the cathedral's obligations. The rest blurred together, a smear of incense and sleepless nights. I rose each day with the best of intentions and lost myself by noon, my mind gnawed by the same old hunger. I kept my head down, performed my duties to the best of my ability, and told myself I was getting better, even as the urge to see *her* grew into a pressure behind my eyes, a tension in my core that begged for release.

I wouldn't go back. It was the lie I spun last Friday, and the Friday before, and every single Friday since midsummer. This week, my resolve lasted until four o'clock, when Quasimodo found me in our tiny kitchen and signed, *Faire tonight?* His face was neutral, still bruised from our last argument, but hope was there, stubborn and fragile.

No. The word burned on my tongue, but I couldn't bring myself to say it aloud. I should tell him it was too dangerous, that the market crawled with guards, that the Church had eyes everywhere, even ones that would report us. I watched the way his hands shook as he poured tea, and caved. *Yes.* I said aloud and signed for good measure, and the way my son's face lit up was worth it.

After last week's altercation, I made an internal promise, one I refused to quickly go back on: I would always say yes to him, even if it ruined us both.

Dressing in my plainest clothes, I bound myself tighter than usual, then shrugged on my heavy cloak reserved for errands that required anonymity. It was the only garment I owned that allowed me to disappear, to move through the city as a shadow instead of a spectacle. My hair, a dead giveaway given its color, was hidden beneath the cloak's heavy hood. To the rest of the world, I looked like any other penitent running errands for the Church. Quasimodo wore a scarf over his mouth and a hood so deep it swallowed his head. We made a sorry pair, skulking through the cathedral's back corridors before using the trademen's entrance to slip into the street.

Outside, the air was razor-sharp, the last light of day already swallowed by the low clouds. I kept my face down, hands jammed in my pockets, and let Quasimodo lead. He knew the route by heart, ducking through alleys and across the bridge with confidence that betrayed just how often we ventured this way. I followed, trying not to think about what could happen if we got caught, nor of any of the numerous forms such an unmasking could take. I was, in every sense, a fraud: a woman in a man's coat, an archdeacon with a head full of blasphemy, and a parent who couldn't keep her promises straight. I tried not to think about the way my body felt in this borrowed state, how the constant pressure of my bindings and the weight of the cloak combined into a strange, bracing comfort. If I could live in that in-between forever—neither seen nor unseen, neither man nor woman, neither saint nor sinner—I might finally find peace.

But it couldn't be, just as we couldn't linger here.

We reached the far side of the river as the market's lanterns came to life. The crowd was already thick, the air alive with the slap of boots and the clatter of vendors hawking their wares. Guards were there, of course, posted at every junction, their eyes flat and hungry, but they paid us no mind. I kept my head down and followed Quasimodo, who craned his neck at every booth, his hands already signing with excitement: a baker selling loaves of bread so fresh they still steamed, a girl with her hair braided into a crown of living violets, and a juggler catching knives. I envied the abandon with which Quasimodo took in the world, and the ease with which he moved through it, never doubting his right to be.

We stopped at the nut vendor first. Quasimodo insisted on sampling every flavor before settling on his customary cone of candied almonds, then offered me the first bite. I took it, the sugar crunching between my teeth. The world was loud here, brighter and warmer than the cathedral's chill, and for a moment I let myself believe in the fiction of normalcy. Just a parent and her son on an evening stroll, nothing to hide, nothing to fear.

But it never lasted. The further we pressed through the crowd, the more I remembered myself: the manner my hips curved beneath the cloak, the way my hands were too small, and how my voice was too soft when I dared to speak. I watched how the men around me inhabited their bodies without care or thought, how their laughter carried, how their steps took up space. I watched the women, too, with their easy grace, their voices pitched higher, their movements fluid and graceful. I didn't fit with either—always hovering at the margins, not quite one or the other. I was not a man, not a woman, not a parent by blood, nor a pious soul by nature. I was myself—and that self was unacceptable.

We made our way to the square's center, where the makeshift stage was already set for the night's performances. Quasimodo edged closer, eager for a better view. I hung back, positioning myself at the edge of a pillar, half-concealed in the crowd. The Embermage would be on soon. I sensed the subtle shift in the air, the way the crowd's anticipation spiked and stilled, as if someone had drawn a blade amidst the throng.

The stage was little more than a raised platform ringed with torches that spat and hissed in the wind. Behind it, a curtain of midnight blue hung from a taut rope, fluttering with every gust. The crowd pressed in, shoulder to shoulder, their faces upturned and hungry. I watched as the opening act, a pair of acrobats, their limbs entwined like vines, tumbled and spun, drawing polite applause.

When the acrobats finished, the torches along the stage guttered low, as if bowing to a power greater than their own… and they were. A hush swept the square: the crowd's anticipation, the heat of a hundred bodies leaning forward, the flicker of something wild and holy poised to descend. The torches flared, casting rippling shadows, and *she* appeared.

The Embermage stepped from the darkness in a ripple of color, her skirt crimson and gold, her bare arms gleaming as if burnished by the very element she commanded. Her hair was unbound tonight, a torrent of black coils that caught the firelight and fractured it into a thousand points. But it was not her hair, nor her umber skin, nor her radiance that caused my jaw to drop.

It was the scarf.

A new prop draped over her shoulders. Its color was impossible to name, shifting from indigo to plum to the blue of a bruise, depending on the angle. The scarf clung to her as she moved, catching the light, creating the illusion that she was both clothed and nude. She toyed with it as she paced the stage, letting it coil around her wrist and neck, slipping it through her fingers, then wound it tight around her palm, so that the flame that followed seemed to bloom from the cloth itself. The crowd gasped, and she smiled; a promise and a dare.

I couldn't look away. Not for a second, not as Quasimodo returned to my side and tugged at my sleeve, his hands signing in frantic delight. The Embermage owned the stage, every inch of it, every pair of eyes. But her movements were different tonight—less showy, less eager to please. She was almost predatory, drawing out each gesture as if savoring the effect it had on those watching. The scarf became an extension of her. She let it trail behind her before snapping it forward, sending a spray of sparks into the air. She looped it around her waist, her thigh, her throat, letting the fire chase its path, burning but never devouring. It was a performance of control, of seduction, of power held and withheld and unleashed.

It struck me that she was looking for someone. Not in the way a performer seeks applause, but the way a hunter seeks its mark. Her eyes found the crowd, but never lingered on any face for long. I watched, desperate, as her eyes swept the square in slow, deliberate arcs, always missing me by a hair. *I want her to find me.* The thought came unbidden, so suddenly I couldn't have repressed it. I wanted it so much I could taste it, like the metallic tang of blood on my tongue as I bit it to keep from crying the only name of hers I knew. I pressed closer to the pillar, heart pounding, and prayed—*Lord help me*—that she would look my way.

The Embermage moved with a slowness that was almost cruel. She teased the flame from her palm, let it sputter and die before conjuring it again, brighter and hotter. The scarf shimmered in the torchlight, changing color with every twist of her body. She let it slide across her bare shoulders, down the small of her back, then caught it in her teeth, biting down just hard enough that the crowd shivered as one. She spun, the scarf trailing behind like a comet's tail, and the fire leapt to follow, painting the air with ribbons of gold and orange. The crowd was silent now, transfixed. I was, too.

It was torture, a slow torment that made every second of watching her feel like being made to kneel on broken glass. I couldn't decide if it was agony or ecstasy, or if the difference truly mattered.

She was beautiful, a kind of beauty that dared you to look away then punished you for it, but it wasn't solely that which made her so captivating. It was the way she moved through the world as if it owed her not just survival, but joy. It was the audacity of her freedom, her refusal to be anything less than exactly herself, and that was what twisted the knife in me. I watched her with a hunger that went deeper than the flesh, a longing so sharp it bordered on hatred. I wanted to possess her, yes, but more than that, I wanted to *be* her. I, too, wanted to exist and not apologize for it. To be seen, wholly and without shame.

Instead, I cowered, half-hidden in shadow, every inch of me bound, barricaded, and terrified.

The Embermage's dance built itself slowly, the scarf wound around her body, trailing behind her as she stalked the edge of the stage. Her eyes swept the perimeter of the crowd, searching, flicking past me. I must have made some involuntary movement—a shift, a gasp—because, for the first time, her gaze jerked back and pinned me where I stood.

My body turned to glass. The world narrowed to the space between us, the distance measured in heartbeats, in the shallow rise and fall of my chest. The Embermage's eyes widened for a fraction of a second before her mouth curved in a slow, private smile. Not the flirtatious grin she gave the crowd, but something more intimate— dangerous, almost cruel in its specificity. For an instant, I felt like the only person in Paris, and she was looking at *me*.

She broke away, spinning into a new sequence, but I couldn't move. Each step she took was a message, a cipher I couldn't hope to crack, but the answer was there in the marrow of my bones. The scarf became a leash, a whip, a caress. She draped it over her arm, then wound it around her throat, arching her back so that every line of her body was thrown into sharp relief. The fire followed, flickering along the edge of her hip, her breast, her collarbone. The crowd shivered in time with her movements, but I stood paralyzed, throat thick, unable to look away for even a heartbeat.

Mid-spin, she paused. Just for a moment, but enough that the crowd's murmur swelled, uncertain. Her gaze swept the square, slower this time, hunting, and when it found me again, it didn't let go.

The world held its breath. There was no denying it now, and it wasn't an accident—this connection, this recognition, the weight of her attention pinning me to the ground. The crowd, the torches, the city, all of it faded. There were only the two of us, strung together across the impossible distance, two points on a line no one but us could see. My heart hammered so violently I thought I might faint. She *saw* me. Not the mask, not the borrowed coat, not the false shape I forced myself into for all these years.

Me.

She held my gaze for a single, excruciating second, long enough for the edges of my vision to blur, long enough for heat to crawl up my neck and stain my cheeks. With a wicked flick of her wrist, she snapped the scarf through the air and spun away, breaking the spell. The crowd exhaled, laughter and applause swelling as The Embermage bowed low, the scarf pooling at her feet like a puddle of midnight. I let out a breathless, shaky sound that might have been a laugh or a sob, and reached for Quasimodo's arm, needing to anchor myself to something real, something solid.

He gazed up at me, eyes wide and bright, hands already moving to sign, *Did you see that? She looked at you.*

I shook my head, lips pressed together so tight I tasted blood. *No,* I signed back with shaking fingers. *It was just part of the show.*

He gave me a glance, one I'd seen a hundred times before: equal parts exasperation and pity, as if he couldn't decide whether to argue or let me drown in my own denial. Instead, he tugged my sleeve, pulling me away from the stage, away from the roaring crowd, away from the heat that still radiated from the torches and the memory of her eyes burning into mine.

We stumbled through the market, the world blurring around the edges. The sharp scent of roasting chestnuts, the clang of steel on stone, the laughter of children, the endless babble of a world that had no idea what just happened. I let Quasimodo guide me, let him chatter in sign about the show, about the scarf, about the way the fire moved. I nodded, made the right noises, but my mind was a chaos of heat and dread and the sick, bright thrill of having been seen.

We made it to the edge of the market before I realized I was trembling, clutching the folds of my cloak with white-knuckled hands. The air was colder here, the wind snapping off the river and stinging my cheeks. I wanted to linger, to let the night swallow me whole, but Quasimodo was already halfway across the bridge, his stride purposeful and quick. I hurried to catch up, the city blurring past in a streak of light and noise.

We said nothing as we crossed the river. I tried to focus on the rhythm of my footsteps, on the clutch of my bindings, on the dull ache in my jaw from clenching it so hard. But all I could see was her: her eyes locking onto mine, her smile a blade pressed to my throat.

She'd sliced me open without even touching me.

I barely remembered the rest of the walk home, only that the city seemed to stagger with me, every stone and shadow echoing the storm in my chest. We made it back to Notre Dame in record time, Quasimodo silent the whole way, eyes huge and dark beneath his hood. I let him in first, ushered him up the stairs, and when he hesitated outside his door, I signed, *Goodnight. I love you.* He replied in kind, his movements slow, as though the night's spell had numbed him too. Then he slipped inside, closing the door with a soft click.

I stood in the corridor, breath shallow, the cold sweat on my back already drying and tightening my skin. The cathedral was quieter than I'd ever known it, every footstep echoing with obscene clarity. I made my way to my chambers, locked the door, and drew the heavy curtain tight. The fire had gone out in the grate, but I didn't bother to relight it. I peeled off my cloak, my shirt, and my bindings, working in silence and haste as if I could outrun what had already happened.

I dropped to my knees.

The stone was cold, biting into my bones, but I welcomed the pain. I clasped my hands together and pressed my forehead to the floorboards, reciting the prayers of contrition I learned as a child.

The words were a lifeline, a thin thread to keep me from drowning in the memory of that moment. Her eyes on mine, the knowledge that she'd seen me, not just the body I wore but the ruin inside. I rattled through the prayers faster, desperate to bury the memory beneath the weight of ritual. When my tongue tripped over the Latin, I opened my eyes and stared at the grain of the wood, vowing not to rise until I purged the hunger from my body.

It wasn't enough.

The ache in my chest turned to a low, steady burn, and I knew from experience that prayer alone would never kill it. I knew what I had to do, even as I recoiled from the thought: the old penance, the one I swore off but never quite abandoned, the only ritual that ever made me feel clean.

So I rose, hands shaking, and crossed to my trunk, pulled it open, and retrieved the scourge. The leather was stiff from disuse, the knots at its end cured to a hardness that would split skin on the first blow. I stood, stripped to the waist, and in the wan candlelight, I saw my reflection in the window: a pale, spectral thing, ribs like prison bars, hair shorn too close, eyes rimmed with sleeplessness. A woman only in the technical sense, an archdeacon only by the grace of a Church that loathed every deviation of my body and soul.

Kneeling by the bed, I braced my left arm against the stone, and let the first lash fall. The sound was a whisper, but the pain was immediate, bright and clarifying. I counted, as always, in Latin—one for every decade of the rosary, another for each unconfessed sin. The first few strokes were nothing, the old numbness settling in like a familiar guest. But the next cut deeper, breaking through the callus, the pain brightening until it threatened to overtake thought. I relished it, welcomed it, made it holy. My breath came in ragged gasps, sweat slicking my back even as the skin split and the first beads of blood welled up. I pictured her as

I did it—The Embermage, her arms raised in the firelight, her eyes still fixed on mine, the heat of her gaze more damning than any lash.

The room grew thick with the scent of iron and old candlewax, the smoke from the market still ghosting my hair and clothes. I lost track of the count, lost track of time itself, until the world narrowed to the white-hot point of discipline, a crucible in which I hoped—always—that the impurity might burn away at last.

But even after my arm failed, after the scourge slipped from my fingers and clattered to the floor, the hunger remained. Worse, it had changed. It was no longer just for her, or for the life denied me, but for an annihilation so complete it would leave nothing of the self behind. I pressed my bleeding back to the cold floor, and let my head thump against the boards. I closed my eyes and waited for the world to shrink down to nothing, but it never did. The memory of her clung to me like a fever. My skin prickled with sweat, the nape of my neck sticky and raw, the air in the room growing thick and sour with each ragged breath.

A strange, bitter tang filled my mouth and nose; a sharp, acrid scent, like burnt sugar and dried blood. I barely registered it at first, too lost in the aftermath, but it grew until it was all I could taste, all I could breathe. The hairs on my arms rose, though the room was freezing, and I became aware of a subtle shift in the air, a pressure at the base of my skull. For a moment I thought I'd overdone it, that I would faint. It wouldn't have been the first time.

But I didn't. I pressed my cheek to the floor and stared into the darkness beneath my bed, waiting for the pain to crest and break. The shadows there seemed to pulse and writhe, crawling up the wall and pooling in the corners.

I blinked, thinking it was a trick of the candlelight, but the shadows didn't retreat. They thickened, peeling away from the corners of the room, their edges blurring and softening into something more like smoke than shadow. They moved with a slow, deliberate purpose—not like the random flickering of firelight, but like something alive, drawn to the rhythm of my ragged breaths.

A choked sob escaped my throat. I tried to push myself up, to scramble away, but my muscles refused to obey, seized by a terror so profound it felt like a physical weight. The tang in the air was stronger now, and the room grew colder, the warmth of the hearth swallowed by this encroaching darkness. The shadows crept closer, swirling at the edge of my vision, their forms indistinct yet present.

They weren't demons. They were specters of my own making, born from the filth of my desire. They were the shape of my sin given form, and they came to claim me. One tendril, darker than the rest, reached for me. It brushed against the raw, bleeding skin of my back, and the touch was not one of fire, but of smoke and ash. It didn't hurt.

It was a caress.

A scream tore from my throat, raw and animalistic, a sound with no prayer or plea. The world tilted, the last of my strength giving way as the darkness rushed in to swallow me whole. My final, waking thought was not of God, nor of penance, but of the impossible green of her eyes, and the chilling certainty that she sent these shadows to fetch me, to drag my soul back to her fire.

I collapsed on the floor, back still bleeding, and let the night claim me.

IV. THE TRYST

Esmeralda

It was unfair how easily Isabelle could unravel my body while my mind refused to stay tethered to the room.

I sprawled across my tangled sheets, her mouth busy along my thigh. Desperate for a distraction, to feel something real, the moment I stepped off stage, I dragged my friend-turned-occasional-lover to my bed last night. She was more than happy to oblige. We went several rounds in the darkness, and several more this morning, but no matter how many orgasms she gave me, or I gave her, all I could do was stare at the ceiling and try to recall the look in the silver-haired stranger's eyes as the scarf wound through my fingers. The perfect prop, as I knew it would be. Even now, with Isabelle's lips tracing patterns along my skin, with the heat of her fire magic summoning mine, all I could see was *him*. All I could hear was the scandalized hush of the crowd as we locked gazes through the smoke. All I could feel was the heat in his eyes, too bright and raw to be anything but genuine.

"Esme, focus." Isabelle's voice cut through my daydream. She bit, too hard, and I wondered if she drew blood. Legs weren't technically off-limits for marks, so long as my skirts would cover said marks, but she got close to where they wouldn't be. "You always do this," she said, sitting up, hands on her hips as her breasts brushed my knee. "If you're bored, just say so."

"I'm not bored," I lied. "I'm… tired. Last night ran long." I rolled over, letting the cotton blanket slip from my shoulders, and gave an apologetic half-smile. Isabelle was beautiful: full-lipped, sharp-cheeked, a tangle of brunette curls spilling to her waist. I wanted to want her as I once had, to give her the attention she so desperately craved. But all I could muster was an ill-timed laugh at the memory of Henrietta's gossip, and a stubborn fixation on the stranger's gaze pressed to the back of my neck.

Isabelle scoffed. "It didn't run *that* long."

"Didn't it?" I replied, trying but failing to close my eyes and see anything other than the silver-haired man's shape cowering behind that pillar.

"Esme." Isabelle's hands pressed into my hips, pinning me in place. "I know that look. You're not here at all, are you?"

I blinked, and there was the ceiling: water stains, a cobweb, the shadow from the neighbor's gutter dancing across the plaster. Isabelle's lips were soft as they brushed mine, but the stranger's eyes lingered in my mind. I tried to summon Isabelle's taste, the way her hair smelled after a morning in the bakery, the little gasp she made when I bit her lower lip. It was all there—familiar, safe, almost comforting. But it wasn't enough.

I rolled her onto her back, hoping momentum might carry me somewhere closer to the present, but Isabelle only laughed as I pinned her arms above her head. "You're not fooling anyone," she said, her breath warm in my ear. "Who is he?"

I hesitated. "No one."

"Liar." She arched her back, her body a long, elegant line beneath me, but her eyes were sharp. "You only get like this when you're obsessed."

I wanted to protest, to insist it was strategy—just a game, a ploy to lure the stranger back to my stage or my bed or both—but Isabelle would see through that. She always had.

"It's not like that," I tried again, softer this time. "I just… he's not what you think."

Isabelle rolled her eyes. "I don't care what you do, Esme. Just don't lie to me about it." She yanked me down for another kiss, deep and bruising, and for a moment I let myself be swallowed by her. My hands roamed her body, mapped every familiar rise and fall, every freckle and scar I'd once memorized with my tongue. She moaned— the sound soft and needy—and I clung to it. Maybe if I held on tightly enough, I could drown out everything else.

But it was no good. Even as she pulled my hand between her legs, guiding my fingers to where she was wet and wanting, my mind was elsewhere. I pictured the way the stranger's eyes fixed on me, the way his lips parted in shock, the tremor that ran through him as if the scarf's violet shimmer lashed through his soul. I pressed my palm harder, drawing a gasp from Isabelle, but to me, it was the stranger's mouth I claimed, the stranger's hands I pinned. I pictured him in the aftermath, the way he staggered from the crowd, his face flushed with something more than embarrassment, his eyes wide as he fled, ruined and desperate.

There was a violence to the memory that thrilled me, a helplessness I wanted to taste again and again. I wondered if he went home and prayed for forgiveness, or if he spent the night in torment, writhing in sheets still stinking of sweat and guilt. I wondered if he let himself surrender to the desire that haunted him, the thing I saw burning behind his careful mask—even if it meant splintering his faith to pieces.

The thought made me shiver. Isabelle noticed, lifting her hips to meet my hand. "See?" she whispered, half-laughing, half-moaning. "You're thinking about him."

I didn't answer, letting her ride the rhythm, letting her whimper and buck and finally collapse, trembling, beneath me. Even as I kissed her shoulder, her breast, the hollow of her throat, Isabelle didn't say a word. She propped herself up on one elbow, giving me a look so devastatingly clear-eyed I almost had to look away. Silence stretched between us, and she didn't ask me to stay, or to explain, or even to want her. Isabelle had always been practical that way. She gathered the sheets around her and watched me as I stared at the ceiling, trying and failing to piece together the ache inside me.

"You're not coming to market with me today, are you?" she asked, voice soft but not unkind.

I shook my head. "Not today."

She nodded before reaching for her skirt and pulling it on, the fabric clinging to her hips with a practiced twist. For a moment, I wanted to call her back, to prove I could be present if I could just have another chance. But the words caught in my throat, and I let her dress in silence, watched the way she moved with a grace so different from my own. Measured, careful, and never anything less than deliberate.

Isabelle wove her curls into a bun and, before leaving, kissed my forehead. It was a gesture so gentle it left me more raw than the sex did. Then she was gone, her footfalls echoing down the stairwell, the scent of her lingering just long enough to prick at the corners of my eyes.

I lay in the quiet, sheets tangled between my legs, the ache in my hips a reminder of what I could and couldn't feel. Sunlight crept through the warped glass of my window, painting the floorboards a pale gold. The scarf lay draped across the foot of my bed, catching every stray beam of light, every piece of dust. I reached for it, letting the fabric snake between my fingers, feeling the weight of each tiny bead as it slid along my skin.

Wrapping it around my neck and wrist before letting it trail over my bare chest, I imagined the way it must have looked from the crowd: how it caught the attention of the only person in the square I needed to see me. I twisted in front of the mirror—still naked except for the scarf and my mére's necklace—and studied myself. The woman who looked back wasn't The Embermage, she was Esmeralda: tall and lean, brown skin aglow in the late-morning sun, curls wild as always, green eyes bright and... haunted.

I watched in the mirror as I wound the scarf slowly before yanking it back with a flourish, letting it pool in my palm before looping it around my fist. I imagined the silver-haired stranger's throat, how the scarf would look against the sharp line of his jaw, or how he'd shiver when I leaned in, close enough to brush his ear with my breath. I pictured him on his knees, face upturned and eyes wanting, the scarf both a leash and a noose. The fantasy should have been enough to make me laugh, or at least to make me feel in control.

It left me hollow, the echo of my own desire with nowhere to go.

I wanted to see myself as he might: a woman who wielded lust like a weapon, who could command a crowd and break a person's heart with a single look. But the longer I stared, the more my reflection betrayed me. Beneath the mask, I was just a woman who lost too much, who turned longing into a shield because it hurt less than letting anyone else see through the cracks. I pressed my forehead to the mirror, breathing until the glass fogged up, and whispered, "You're not fooling anyone."

Not even yourself.

Unable to bear my tormented reflection, I forced myself to get dressed, every movement feeling like it took twice the effort. The scarf was first—I needed it to smell like me—so I wound it around my neck, letting the ends spill down my chest before reaching for a soft linen shirt and the pair of tailored black breeches that once belonged to my père. I cinched my waist with a wide leather belt, then shrugged on a vest stitched in the deep green favored by the Council, though I left it unbuttoned. My mére's necklace rested at the base of my throat, just above where the scarf glinted in the light. There: armor assembled, performance ready. If I couldn't feel it, I could at least fake looking the part.

I made my way down the stairs, but before my feet hit the landing, there came the clatter of Jules's boots on the tile below. I braced myself, knowing from the sound alone they were pissed. Jules only stomped when they were ready to make a scene.

Sure enough, the moment I rounded the banister, my sibling was there, arms folded, a mug of coffee trembling in one hand. Their eyes hovered over me, the scarf, then back to my face. "You're up early," they said, which was code for *I heard everything last night.* Hardly fair considering I was subjected to Jules and Antoine's rather loud trysts nearly *every* night.

"Insomnia," I replied, breezing past them and into the kitchen. "Or maybe just guilt. Hard to say."

"Isabelle left early." Jules sipped their coffee, lips pursed. "Looked like she'd been crying."

I bristled, but made a show of rummaging through the breadbox. "She's fine."

"Did you dump her?"

"I was never *with* her," I snapped. "We're friends. Friends fuck sometimes."

Jules let that hang in the air before setting down their mug. "You're going to ruin her."

"She's perfectly capable of making her own choices, and last night that choice was me. I made her no promises. She'll survive." I tore off a hunk of bread and popped it in my mouth, chewing so I wouldn't have to answer the next question right away.

Jules didn't bother with subtlety. "Was it the Church man?"

I choked, not expecting *that* question, at least not yet. "What?"

They rolled their eyes. "You think I didn't see you last night? The whole square saw you." Their voice dropped, almost a hiss: "What the fuck was that, with the scarf? I've never seen you be that seductive, not in public. And don't get me started on what you did to that poor man. You undressed him with your eyes in front of half the mages of Paris."

My cheeks flushed. "It's called theater. I thought you of all people would understand."

Jules's laugh was sharp as a blade. "You're not that good an actress, Es. The whole crowd saw what you did. So did the guards. You want to get yourself arrested? Worse?"

I rolled my eyes, but my hand shook on the bread knife. "He's not going to report me. He's not—"

"You know nothing about him," Jules shot across me. "All you know is he shows up week after week, always with his hood pulled low, never saying a word, but staring at you like he wants to eat you alive. That's not a fan, Es. That's a Church spy, and you know it."

I winced. "He's not a spy. He has a kid—"

"Oh, so now you're a stepmother?" Jules's voice remained low, but somehow managed to fill the entire kitchen. "I'm serious. You're playing with fire. *Actual* fire, but worse. These are flames you can't control."

I wanted to scream at them, or maybe myself, but I managed to keep my voice down, not wanting to summon Antoine again. "Don't you dare lecture me about danger. I know exactly what I'm doing, who he is, and what he could do to us if he wanted. But he doesn't, he hasn't, and he won't. He's not like the others."

Jules snorted, but the edge was gone from their anger; in its place was something softer, more brittle. "You think you're the first mage to fall for a pretty Church boy? You think you're the first to believe you're special?"

I shrugged, refusing to meet their eyes. "Maybe I am. Maybe he is. You don't know him."

"You don't know him, either." Jules leaned in, elbows on the table, their gaze suddenly so close it was hard to breathe. "You think you're always running the show, but you're not. You're just the mark. Remember? The Church makes you feel like you're in control, right up until the moment they take everything from you."

I flinched at the memory, because of course I fucking remembered:

the flash of torchlight, the boots on the stairs, the last time anyone in our family believed themselves untouchable. I clamped down on the thought, forcing myself to look up, meeting Jules's warning glare with one of equal intensity. "What if I'm tired of being afraid? What if I want to take something back for once, instead of waiting for them to come for us?"

Jules shook their head. "You sound like Maman when you say things like that."

"Good," I said, surprised by how much I meant it. "Maybe if she had the chance to finish what she started, we wouldn't be hiding like cowards in our own city."

The words landed, heavy and spiteful, but I didn't regret them. I was tired of being the one to apologize, to make myself smaller, to live in fear of the next raid, the next loss. If I was reckless, it was only because every other option had been ripped away—just like Maman.

Jules stood, gathering their mug and rinsing it in the sink. "It's not about whether you survive. It's about what it *costs*. Every time you get close to someone, you give up another piece of yourself. Soon you'll wake up and there won't be anything left."

I searched for a retort, something sharp enough to puncture the awful intimacy of Jules's gaze, but found myself studying their face. They looked older, suddenly, or maybe just more tired than I let myself notice.

"Don't start with me," I said, forcing my voice soft. A truce. "You're not the only one who gets to make bad decisions."

Jules snorted, the sound barely audible. "I never said I was a saint. But at least I don't go looking for ways to get us both killed."

"That's not what this is," I shot back, but the words sounded childish even to me. I dropped my hands to the table, palms flat, willing them to stop trembling. "You *know* why I have to do this. If we don't push back, if we don't make them see us, they'll keep picking us off one by one, just like the Sirots. That's what they want. For us to be scared. When we are, we do the work for them."

Jules's eyes flicked to the window, where the street outside glowed with early afternoon light "You think seducing a Church man will bring them back? Will bring *Maman* back?"

"No," I admitted, "I just want to be the one who chooses what it costs." I stared at my hands, the callouses and scars, the life I built out of ashes, and wished I could articulate any of it better than I just had. But Jules had already retreated, jaw clenched, eyes shuttered. They finished rinsing their mug with unnecessary force before setting it upside down on the drying rack.

"You're a fool, Es," they said, refusing to look at me. "You think you're the only one who lost her. You think you're the only one who remembers what she fought for. But I was there, too. I watched them drag her out. Except I heard her scream for you, not for me." The last words landed like a slap, and I flinched. "So go ahead. Burn everything down, if that's what you want. Just don't pretend you're doing it for anyone but yourself."

I stood so fast my chair toppled, the crash echoing against the kitchen tile. My flames leapt to the surface of my skin, trickling up my palms and responding strongly to my emotion, and it took every ounce of willpower I had to keep them at bay. I wanted to throw something, to break every mug in the cupboard, to shatter the window and let the chill in until it froze us both. Before I could do anything I'd regret, I snuffed my flames, snatched my coat, and bolted outside. The air slapped the heat from my cheeks, the cold so sharp it dulled the edges of my anger. I slammed the door behind me hard enough to rattle the warped wood, and for a second I stood on the stoop, chest heaving, wishing I could combust on the spot and leave nothing but ash for Jules to sweep up.

Marching down the street, my boots echoed on wet stone, my scarf wound tight enough to bite. The chill was brutal, the sort that gnawed at your bones and made you long for fire, but I welcomed it. Let the cold numb me. Maybe then I could stop replaying every word Jules said, every wound disguised as wisdom.

By instinct, my feet took me to the market. It was still early, at least for the market's standards. The vendors were still setting up, lanterns swinging in the pale light, frost crusting the edges of every crate. I drifted through the stalls, hands shoved in my pockets, head down. I wanted to be invisible, but for me, that was impossible.

A few people nodded as I passed—old friends, rivals, even former lovers. Henrietta caught my eye and gave a half-salute with her knitting needles, but I pretended not to see. I didn't trust myself not to break if someone asked Are you all right? Or worse: What did you do this time? There was no good answer to either of those questions.

The market was a different creature in the morning. Without the crowd's noise, everything felt exposed—each empty stall a tiny stage awaiting its performer. Half of them were shuttered, the rest manned by vendors who watched the street with a wariness I hadn't seen since the last round of purges. The sudden disappearance of the Sirots combined with the Church's show of force at last night's performance had been a clear warning, one the market received loud and clear.

Jules's words circled in my head: They take everything from you. It was a warning meant to make me afraid, to make me reconsider the dangerous game I played with the silver-haired stranger. But all it did was conjure the face of Henrietta as she delivered the news days ago. The Sirots. The whole family… gone.

It was an all-too-familiar horror. Another story to be filed away with the dozens of others. Another reason to keep our heads down. But after my fight with Jules, after seeing the raw hunger in the stranger's eyes and the terror in my sibling's, the news felt different. It was a punch to the gut, and a weight I couldn't ignore. My feet carried me away from the market by instinct alone, toward the narrow, winding streets of the weavers' district.

I needed to see it, to stand before the reality Jules was so desperate for me to fear.

The street where the Sirots lived—or rather, used to live— was quiet, the silence smothering the usual hum of life. When the house at last came into view, it was a dark stain on what had once been familiar. It became impossible to breathe as reality all but slapped me in the face. The splintered front door hung from a single, groaning hinge. The windows were shattered, gaping voids that stared with vacant eyes. When I dared to step closer, a shard of glass crunched under my boot. Inside, the chaos was absolute. A loom in the corner lay on its side, its threads cut. On the floor by the hearth lay a small wooden bird, its painted wing cracked, and the sight took my breath away.

The Sirots' youngest daughter clutched a similar-looking toy at the spring festival last year.

My stillness lingered, but not over long. As I picked through the remainder of the ransacked house, my thoughts continued to race. Logically, this should be more than enough to scare me back into hiding. But standing in the heart of the Sirots' stolen life, it wasn't fear that shook me. It was rage, pure and cold. The Sirots had been careful, kept their heads down, followed all the rules— yet this was their reward. The hollowed-out home, the broken bird, the violent silence.

Caution is a lie.

My fingers crept to my throat, closing around the beaded silk of the scarf. In that moment, it was no longer a mere prop. It was a weapon, much like the silver-haired stranger was the perfect door into the heart of the very institution that had done this. I was going to kick it in, even if it ruined me. My path was clear now, stripped of all doubt. Jules and all the others would see a reckless girl chasing a dangerous obsession, leading herself and all others to ruin. My fist tightened: let them.

Let them think I was a fool blinded by desire. I would wield their assumptions like a blade, for my performance, my well-laid trap, was over.

My hunt had just begun.

V. THE TEMPTATION

Claude

I couldn't get the scarf out of my mind.

No matter how many times I recited psalms or how furiously I tended to the bruising on my back, the image persisted. Violet and vibrant, rippling through the air like a streak of lightning. I saw it in the shape of the clouds as I looked out the clerestory windows, in the stains upon the altar cloth, the pooled wax of the candelabra. I even saw it in the robes of a visiting bishop, which, to my horror, I found myself staring at with obsessive intensity. I could not escape the scarf. I could not escape *her*.

The Embermage's performance ruined me. I replayed every second, every flick of her wrist and glimmer of her teeth, every time her gaze swept the crowd and fixated on me. After last week, surely I had seen every possible permutation of her seduction, and with enough suffering and self-inflicted pain, I could cauterize the forbidden desire from my flesh. But there she remained, burning bright, as always.

And now, she had seen *me*.

I spent the better part of the morning locked in my chambers, refusing all visitors, berating myself for the loss of self-control the night before. I went too far, left too many marks. The wounds were still raw, the fabric of my undershirt sticking to the crusted blood, each movement a reminder that I couldn't be trusted with my own flesh. Despite my penance, The Embermage remained there whenever I closed my eyes—her body arching beneath the shroud of violet, the fire glinting off her bare arms, her smile a sin written across her face. She knew what she was doing. She saw how I watched her.

This wasn't just an obsession anymore. It was a sickness, an infection that spread through my mind and sapped my will to resist. I tried to tell myself it was temporary, that I could endure, that each day brought me closer to liberation. But the days only grew longer, the hours more empty. I couldn't bear to face Quasimodo, the boy I swore to protect, when I couldn't even protect myself. I sent him out with errands and barricaded myself in my office, as if a locked door could stop my racing thoughts.

It was midday when the inevitable knock came. I braced for the worst. Father Laurent, perhaps, with a fresh round of scorn or some new flavor of penance. But it was only Brother Matthieu, clutching a sheaf of papers and looking like he'd rather be anywhere else

"Archdeacon," he said. "There's… something you should see."

I closed the ledger I hadn't been reading and waved him in, unwilling to let even the faintest whiff of my humiliation escape into the halls. Matthieu entered, eyes fixed to the floor, and set the documents on my desk. They were reports from the city watch, incident logs from the past fortnight, each stamped with the Prefecture seal. Normally, this was the sort of paperwork I delegated to Laurent or, failing that, ignored entirely.

This morning, I leafed through them with a kind of desperate focus. The words on the page blurred, bleeding into one another, names and locations rendered meaningless by the static in my skull. Only when Matthieu cleared his throat twice did I manage to seize the point.

"We've… been making arrests," he said, his voice so low I had to lean in to hear it. "Not as many as the Bishop wants, but enough to make the market uneasy."

I nodded, feigning authority. "They're mages. They should be uneasy."

He went silent, hands trembling. I tried to recall what I knew of Matthieu: a few years younger than me, clean-shaven and soft, the type of man who would rather copy out a hundred sermons than confront evil in the flesh. He was assigned here last winter, and in all that time, I'd never seen him so much as raise his voice. It was a small, bitter comfort to know I inspired fear in someone.

"Is there more?" I asked, and my voice had a cold edge to it, the one I sharpened for moments of doubt. I had to be cruel, though. It was the only way to keep my mask from slipping.

Brother Matthieu's mouth compressed to a thin, white line. "One of the families, the Sirots on Rue des Martyrs, has not been seen in several days. A few neighbors say they left in the night, but we believe…" He hesitated, as if the rest of the sentence might choke him. "We believe the Captain of the Guard may have intervened. The new one, Phoebus."

The name rang only a faint bell of recognition. After our last Captain had resigned—good riddance, for I'd never liked the old fool—I recalled that a younger, stricter one had been appointed in his place. I'd also heard rumors that he liked to push the limits of his authority, and that even Father Laurent had a hard time keeping him in line. I tapped the stack of reports, fingers drumming a nervous rhythm. "Are the Sirots in custody?"

Matthieu shook his head. "No record. Not in any of the holding cells, at least. But there are… rumors." He swallowed hard. "That they're being kept somewhere else. A new place, off the books."

I kept my face blank, though a chill crawled up my spine as my thoughts raced, trying to piece everything together. *A new place.* That sounded like Laurent, but worse… it sounded like an escalation. And it wasn't within the Church's rights or authority, not even Father Laurent's. We weren't permitted to hold prisoners indefinitely, and we certainly weren't permitted to execute them without trial. So what in God's name had Phoebus done with them?

"You mentioned the family was unaccounted for." It was a fight to keep that icy nonchalance in my voice. "Does that include children, or is it only adults?"

"All members, Archdeacon: there are two children missing, as well as both parents."

Children. Quasimodo's face flashed in my mind's eye as I pictured him behind bars, trembling and alone. My suspicion and rage only grew, but one glance at Matthieu's face told me that if I dared to seem any more interested than I already had, I might well be questioned myself. "Is that all?" I asked, loathing myself for even pretending to care as if missing children's lives meant nothing to me, mages or not.

Matthieu nodded, his relief that I hadn't asked for more almost palpable. "Yes, Archdeacon Frollo."

"Thank you, Brother. Leave the files."

He placed the sheaf at the edge of my desk, hands already retreating. I watched as he left, his footsteps light and quick. In another life, I might have pitied him, but I'd long since run out of pity, even for myself.

I waited for the latch to click shut before I exhaled. *The Sirots.* I remembered them now: the mother, soft-spoken and always wrapped in a shawl, the father who walked with a limp, the two daughters who sometimes sold wildflowers outside the cathedral on Sundays. There were hundreds of mage families in Paris, but a handful set themselves apart by the sheer invisibility of their existence. The Sirots were the sort who never caused trouble, never raised their voices. The sort the world did not notice until it was too late.

I shuffled the papers with numb fingers, searching for meaning in the bureaucratic drivel. The words blurred and reformed, until at last I saw it: a brief, handwritten addendum at the bottom of a page. "*Unconfirmed reports of violence at the Sirot residence. No witnesses willing to testify. All property impounded.*" I could picture how it happened—how efficient it would be, with no one left to protest. How easy to disappear an entire family from the world, especially for a man with as much authority and power as Phoebus, as if the world had never truly seen them in the first place. The Sirots would leave behind no legacy: just a shuttered window, a broken house, perhaps a fading memory in the minds of the people who had known them.

Surely The Embermage would hear of it. I pictured the news traveling through the market, carried on the lips of apothecaries and bards, passed like a curse from stall to stall. I imagined her face hardening, her jaw set with that stubborn defiance I saw both onstage and in my dreams. What would it do to her, to know the city she called home was closing its fist around her and her kind? Would she hide in the shadows? Or would she burn brighter, if only to spit fire in the face of her oppressors?

The thought made my hands shake. I pressed them flat against the desk, willing the tremors to still. For a moment, I let myself imagine what it would be like to meet her in this state: not as a holy woman, not as a warden of the city's virtue, but as someone ruined by her own hunger. Would she laugh, or would she pity me?

I couldn't bear either thought.

Slamming the file shut, I stood, tucked the reports under my arm, and marched from my office. The corridor outside was empty save for a shaft of light from an unshuttered window. I took the spiral stairs two at a time, ignoring the ache in my back, the wet pull of fabric from half-healed skin. I needed to move, to do something with the rage and helplessness that threatened to turn my bones to powder if I sat still. My footsteps echoed, sharp and hollow. Veering left at the crossing, I took the narrow passage that led to the belltower.

Quasimodo was on the north balcony, splayed across the stone ledge, carving an animal into the wood of the balustrade with a dull knife. He didn't notice me at first, but when he did, he jerked upright, the knife nearly tumbling from his hand. He looked wary, but upon seeing my face, concerned.

You're bleeding, he signed, glancing at my shoulder, even though I wore my best attempt at a high-collared shirt and my cloak was fastened tight. My neck must have been flecked with blood, the crust from a scab split by my frantic pace. I pressed a palm to it, annoyed, and tried to smile.

"I'm fine," I said. The words sounded foreign to me, as if they belonged to someone else. I signed it for good measure, but my hands shook, my fingers betraying the lie.

Quasimodo watched me with that unnerving, gentle patience he reserved for me when I was at my worst. He set the knife down, brushing the wood shavings from his shirt, and signed, *What happened?*

Nothing, I replied. *Just a long morning.* I forced myself to breathe. The air up here was sharp, carrying the scent of rain and the distant sweetness of roasting nuts from the market below. I tried to let it fill me up, to sweep out the violence of the last twenty-four hours, but the smell only made me dizzy.

I turned my gaze outward, over the sprawl of the city. The rooftops were sullen and heavy with fog, the market a distant blur of color and movement. I tried to spot the square, the makeshift stage, but from this height, everything bled together. The Embermage was out there, somewhere in the crowd, her silhouette a bright point of color against the drab gray of Paris. I wondered if she ever looked up at the cathedral, if she thought of the people who dwelled in its shadows. If she thought of me.

Quasimodo's hand touched my sleeve, a gentle reminder to stay present. He signed, *Are we going to the faire tonight?*

I hesitated, the words catching in my chest. Part of me wanted to say yes, to promise him the small pleasure of sugared almonds and street magicians and the wild, living magic of the market. But the other part—the part that remembered the Sirots, the unmarked graves, the new Captain who could very well target not just Quasimodo, but my brother Jehan if I gave him any trouble—knew I couldn't risk it. Not with Laurent sniffing at my door, not with every step I took being measured and weighed by a Church eager for the slightest misstep that would lead to my undoing.

No, I signed, keeping my hands steady. *Not tonight.*

Quasimodo's face fell, then brightened with a stubborn spark. He pointed across the city, signing, *That's okay. She will perform even if it rains. The stage has a roof, and I can see it from here.*

The way he said it—so sure, so determined—almost undid me. *He was looking forward to it all week*, I realized. The market, the faire, the little rituals we had built together out of the scraps of our lives. The ache in my throat sharpened to a point. *You have a better view than anyone up here*, I signed, and tried for a smile. *No one will block your sight.*

Quasimodo's hands fluttered. *You'll watch, too?*

I wanted to say yes. I wanted to promise him I would stand at his side, that I wouldn't let the world or the Church or my own sick, gnawing hunger take this from us. But I lied, as I too often did. *Maybe, for a little while. I have work to do.*

He nodded, accepting it with more grace than I deserved, before turning back to his carving—a skill he'd picked up from Jehan. I watched Quasimodo work, just as I had my brother in our childhood, letting the rhythm of the knife and wood fill the silence between us. The shape became clearer as Quasimodo whittled, and a soft gasp escaped me: a tiny bird, its wings unfurled as if caught midflight. It was the painted bird from the Sirot girl's hand, the one she carried every Sunday. He slowed, holding the carving for my inspection. His face was solemn, eyes wide and unreadable.

It's for her, he signed, and for a moment I couldn't breathe. I had no idea how he knew. Perhaps he became aware of the rumors, or perhaps he saw the way I lingered over the news. Perhaps, God help me, he simply understood the world was full of wounds, and that sometimes the only thing to do was make some small thing of beauty from the shards.

Reaching for the carving, I turned it over in my palm, savoring the blunt warmth of a thing made with love. I thought of the Sirots, vanished in a night. I thought of the market, emptying as the guards closed in. I thought of The Embermage, wondering if she'd been affected by the raids, by the violence that ravaged her community.

Of course she had. Guilt gnawed at me even before I finished the foolish thought, for I was complicit in it. I may not have wielded a blade myself, but the fact remained that I was no better than Phoebus was through my silence, my helplessness. More quips caught on my tongue. I *should* tell Quasimodo to stay away from the market, to never look down from this tower, to keep his heart locked away from the world's cruelty. But that wasn't what I promised him. He deserved no less than the world and all its joys.

Instead, I handed him its pain.

Quasimodo pressed the bird into my hand, gentle and insistent, tearing me from my thoughts. *For you to give her*, he signed, his movements so precise I could not mistake them even if I wanted to.

I closed my fist around the carving, feeling its wings dig into my palm. "Thank you," I said, voice rough and weary. He nodded, turned away, and busied himself with the next scrap of wood. I lingered, watching him work, searching his face for any sign of resentment, any trace of the anger I so richly deserved. But there was nothing. Just the focused concentration of a boy who wanted, more than anything, to make something that would last.

When I could trust myself again, I left him there, descending the stairs with the carved bird clenched tight. Retreating to my office, I pulled the door shut behind me and slumped in my chair. The carved bird felt as heavy as lead as I traced its shape, running my thumb over its rough, unfinished wings. There was comfort in its imperfection. I set it on my desk, next to the stack of reports, and watched it for a while, as if it might take flight at any moment.

Outside, the sky darkened. Wind battered the stained glass, and from somewhere in the nave, a draft carried the scent of incense and rain. I stared at the bird until my vision blurred, until the world shrank to a single point of focus: the ache in my chest, the endless hunger, the certainty that I was one misstep away from annihilation.

I should have gone to confession. I should have written Laurent, or at the very least, found some task worthy of my station to occupy my hands, my mind. But I could do nothing. I stared at the bird, and then at the sheaf of papers, and then at my own blood staining the cuff of my sleeve.

Eventually, I forced myself to read. Not the reports, but a letter—one I'd been avoiding for days, as if it contained a curse that would only activate when my eyes crossed the first line. It was from Laurent, written in his fastidious, looping hand, and folded thrice to fit beneath my office door in the night. I broke the seal and read:

Archdeacon Frollo,

It has come to my attention that your conduct of late has been erratic. Several of your brethren have reported absences from prayer, neglect of your canonical obligations, and an overreliance on corporal penance. I am told your son has been seen at the markets past curfew, and that your presence was noted in unsavory company.

I need not remind you how fragile your position is, nor the dangers of exposing yourself, and by extension the Church, to the city's many temptations. I have observed, with some dismay, the growing attention you have attracted from the Bishop. He is not known for his patience or forgiveness. I urge you, as your confessor and friend, to remember your vows.

You are treading a dangerous path. Consider this your first—and final—warning.

In Christ,

Father Laurent

I read it twice, then a third time, searching for any trace of warmth in the words. There was none, which wouldn't have surprised my brother Jehan in the slightest. Laurent had always been measured, but at least to me, this was the closest he'd ever come to making an outright threat. That type of wrath was usually reserved for Jehan, but my brother had left the church years ago. A chill shot up my spine. Was I about to be next?

I stared at the closing line—*Consider this your first and final warning*—and the mere thought of it being acted upon radiated up my arms, burrowing under my skin. This was how it started. One report, one letter, and soon the walls would close in. I would be called to account, and when they discovered the truth of my deception, the Church would swallow me whole.

Just as they had with Jehan.

Pressing the heel of my hand to my eyes, I tried in vain to banish the thought, but my mind raced ahead to the next performance, the next slip, the moment they would drag me before the Bishop and demand a confession I could never give. I pictured myself on my knees, the words caught in my throat, Laurent's face cold and remote as he pronounced his sentence. Frantically, desperately, I composed my apology, my plea for leniency, my promise to do better. Even now, I could taste the lie of it.

A knock at the door, sharp and insistent, made me jolt so hard the letter slipped from my hand. I snatched it up, folded it, and shoved it beneath a ledger before calling out, "Enter."

The door swung open with a gust of cold and the scent of wet wool. Mercedes. My oldest… friend wasn't the right word, but it wasn't wrong, either. We'd been close since we were children. Sometimes *too* close. Despite swearing one another off on a multitude of occasions, we always found our way back to one another.

She stood in the threshold, red hair damp with rain, her shawl clinging to her shoulders, revealing white freckled skin. Her eyes were a cold, clear blue that pierced straight through my layers of pretense. Mercedes closed the door behind her with deliberate care, then regarded me in silence, as if waiting for me to confess whatever crime she caught me in. It wouldn't be the first time.

I stood, smoothing the front of my shirt, and tried not to wince at the pull of scabbed over skin. "Yes?"

Mercedes's gaze snapped toward the bird on my desk, then to my face. "You missed vespers," she said, her voice as level as mine. "Laurent noticed."

"Does no one remember I have a son?" I snapped, harsher than intended, but I quickly caught myself. "I… I'm sorry. I was with Quasimodo. You can ask him yourself."

Mercedes's lips quivered, the barest ghost of a smile. "I did. He claims you were with him for less than an hour, and that you spent most of it staring at the market." She shrugged off her shawl and stalked across the office. "He also says you haven't eaten since yesterday, and that you're bleeding through your collar again."

"It's nothing," I said, but she was already at my side, tilting my chin back with two fingers to examine the wound. The press of her thumb against my jaw sent a jolt through me. I tried to pull away, but Mercedes's grip tightened, her eyes searching my face for the lie she knew I would tell.

"Always so damn stubborn," she muttered, but I didn't miss the smirk playing on her lips. "Sit."

I obeyed only because I didn't possess the energy to argue. Mercedes rummaged in the cabinet by the hearth, producing a cloth and a small bottle of alcohol. She dabbed the cloth with the liquid, then pressed it to my neck. The sting was sharp, but I didn't flinch, only biting my lip. I'd been through worse.

Mercedes dabbed and pressed, her breath hot against my cheek. Her scent was as I remembered: clove, rain, and a faint, smoky musk she favored even before she left the convent. I swallowed, determined not to let her see how much her touch rattled me. The Embermage's scent was nothing like hers, and still, in my mind, the two tangled together, violet and fire against the old, forbidden comfort of Mercedes's hands on my body.

"You should be more careful." She said as she wiped the blood away, her tone brisk but not unkind. "The Bishop is watching."

"I know," I said, unable to meet her eyes. "It's under control."

Mercedes laughed sharply. "If this is control, I'd hate to see you unraveled."

I bristled, but her fingers at my collarbone were gentler than her words. She set the bottle down, then brushed my hair aside, exposing the raw line of last night's penance. "You're getting sloppy," she said, and though her words were meant to scold, there was a note of something else—admiration, perhaps, or a kind of nostalgia for the old days when we shared such wounds like secrets.

Mercedes's hands lingered at my throat, her thumb pressing the pulse there, as if to test whether I was truly alive. She let go only when satisfied, the ghost of her touch burning hotter than my sins ever could. She stepped back, eyes narrowed, searching for the right words to wound me, to draw me out, to remind me of who I was before all this.

For once, she didn't utter a word. She simply looked at me, the silence between us heavy as rain in the air. Then she crossed to the door, turned the lock, and drew the curtain over the glass. The scrape of the bolt was thunder in my bones, for her intentions were crystal clear.

"We shouldn't," I said, my voice barely above a whisper. "Not here. Not now."

Mercedes laughed again. This time, there was no sharpness, only a hunger so raw it made my hands tremble. She advanced—the curve of her mouth cruel and sweet—and knelt before my chair, hands on my knees, nails digging through the fabric.

"Tell me to stop."

My hands braced against the armrests, knuckles white with uncertainty, but Mercedes only pressed closer, the weight of her body warm between my knees. She looked up as if I were the last light in the world, her breath shallow, lips parted with the faintest tremor. I saw her like this before, years ago, in the shadowed alcoves of the convent, in the half-lit corridors of the cathedral after curfew. She was always first to dare, first to shatter the illusion of holy detachment, and I—weak-willed, prideful, and desperate for absolution—had always followed, always let the sin drag me under.

Tonight, I *wanted* to refuse her. To prove that I could, at last, be more than a collection of appetites. But she knew me too well. She pressed her cheek to my thigh, thumb stroking the inside of my knee through the thin cloth of my trousers, and murmured, "Tell me to stop, Claude."

I couldn't.

My fingers threaded through her damp hair, pulling her to me. She smiled against my thigh, and I felt the heat of her breath even through two layers of fabric. The old hunger was there, insistent and wild, but it was nothing compared to the inferno that blazed in the periphery of my mind, violet and gold and always beyond my reach. I needed to extinguish it, or at least drown it in another, lesser fire.

Mercedes made it easy. She always had.

She moved with ruthless precision, her hands sliding up my legs, bunching the fabric at my hips and holding me in place. I seized control before she could do much else—grabbing her wrists, pinning them together in one hand. Something flickered in her eyes when she looked up: not fear, but anticipation so keen it bordered on pain.

"Not here," I said again. I yanked her to her feet, spun her so she faced the window, and pressed her palms flat to the glass. Rain spattered the leaded panes, running down toward the cathedral's stone walls. We were both visible in the reflection staring back at us: Mercedes, flushed and open-mouthed, and me, hair mussed, eyes wild, a streak of my own blood at her jaw where I marked her.

It was that image, myself terrifying and monstrous, Mercedes ruined and radiant, that undid me. I pressed my body to hers, pinning her, caging her, feeling her shudder beneath the press of my hips. She arched her back, a willing offering, and I took her as if I could fill the hollow inside me with her warmth alone. My hands were rough, unyielding. I wanted to bruise her, to make her ache in all the places I did, to leave some evidence that I could ravage the world as it had ravaged me.

Mercedes moaned through her teeth, the sound nearly lost beneath the rain, and I clapped a hand over her mouth. She bit my palm, gentle at first, then harder when I didn't flinch. I dug my free hand into her hair, wrenching her head back so she was forced to look at our reflection. "Watch," I hissed, and she did, eyes wide and wet, her breath fogging the glass.

I bent her forward, pressed my mouth to her nape, and tasted the salt and clove of her skin. Mercedes shuddered, hands splaying against the slick glass as if she could steady herself against the world. Against *me*. She was a fool to even think she could, for she of all people knew how badly I wanted to break her, remold her, make her remember me in every ache and echo. But even as I ground my hips against the curve of her ass, even as I pressed my teeth to the tender skin beneath her jaw, it wasn't her body I saw or even felt.

It was The Embermage's.

Her violet scarf trailed through my mind, a ghost limb, winding itself around my wrist. I squeezed Mercedes's neck with one hand, just enough to make her gasp. In that half-choked sound there came the hush of a crowd, the crackle of fire, the sharp intake of breath as The Embermage's eyes locked onto mine from across the square. I pressed Mercedes harder to the window, my own breath now steaming up the glass, and in the blurred reflection I saw a stranger: hair wild, eyes bloodshot, mouth twisted in something not quite pain nor pleasure.

My hands shook as I unfastened Mercedes's skirt, yanking it over her hips. She wore nothing beneath—of course she didn't—and the sight of her bare flesh would have unraveled me once. I ran my palm down the length of her thigh as she braced herself against the window. Pressing my fingers between her legs, I found her slick and ready. She gasped again, this time so loudly it threatened to shatter the glass. I clamped my hand over her mouth once more, smothering the sound, and in the back of my mind I heard the crowd hush, saw the flash of purple and gold, the way The Embermage commanded silence with a glance.

Mercedes bucked against my hand and I obliged her with a ruthlessness I hadn't shown in years. I moved my fingers inside her, driving her toward the edge with single-minded purpose. She clawed at the window, nails squealing on the glass, and I twisted my wrist, forcing her to look up, to see the wreck she had made of herself in the reflection. Her body went rigid, then convulsed, her breath hot against my palm as she orgasmed. She sagged against the window, limp and powerless.

It should have satisfied me. It should have been enough.

But I wanted—*needed*—more.

"Look at you, coming before I've barely touched you." The words came out like a threat, and Mercedes shivered, a tremble running through her. I bit her shoulder hard enough to leave a bruise, and she whimpered, the sound escaping from under my hand. I could have spent hours tormenting her, making her suffer for every slight, all the times she had the power to undo me with a glance. But tonight I hungered for something greater, something I didn't dare name, and she was simply the vessel I used to pour it out.

I forced her to her knees, the stone floor cold and unyielding, her skirt bunched at her hips, hair wild about her shoulders. I gripped her jaw, forcing her to look at me, and for an instant her eyes burned with defiance, the old dare. I remembered when we were young together, how we'd sneak into the crypts after curfew, daring one another to touch, to taste, to see how far we could go before the fear of God or the hands of another sister would stop us. Mercedes had never been the first to flinch.

Not even now. She knelt there, waiting for me to move, her breath heaving. Mercedes was beautiful, truly, but not in the way that haunted me, not in the way that would ever satisfy that deeper ache. I wanted to desire her, but everything inside me belonged to the stage, to the fire, to the impossible woman who could never be mine. I could have kissed Mercedes, could have taken her apart with tenderness, but I didn't. Instead, I gripped her by the hair and pulled her head back, to see the hunger there and know it wasn't for her.

She made a sound, half-laugh, half-moan, and I let her savor the pain. If she wanted to be ruined—and I wanted to ruin something, anything, so long as it wasn't myself—so be it. I balled her hair tighter, my other hand tracing the line of her throat, then her collar, then the sharp edge of her jaw. She shuddered, eyes fluttering closed, and I slapped her hard enough to leave a mark. Her mouth fell open, and I slipped my thumb between her lips, letting her bite down, letting her taste the sweat of my skin and the faint, metallic tang of my blood.

The pain was clean and welcome, and it only spurred me on. Sliding my hand from her jaw to her throat, my thumb pressed until it fluttered beneath her skin. She stared up at me, lips parted, and I let myself imagine it was The Embermage kneeling there—her gaze molten, her tongue tracing the moisture on my palm, her body desperate to be burned.

The fantasy took root, feverish and raw, and I leaned into it. I closed my eyes and saw her: the dancer, the temptress, the woman who could ignite a crowd with her fiery dance. I imagined her on her knees, hair a dark halo, the scent of violets and smoke clinging to her skin. She would not beg, not The Embermage. She would look up at me with scorn and hunger, daring me to take what I wanted, daring me to break her. Would she crumble, or would she fight me every step of the way, turning pain into power, her shame into something holy?

Lightning flashed, illuminating the office in a jagged blaze of white, and the thunder that followed was so close it rattled the glass. The storm had begun slowly, but now every window trembled in its wake. I barely registered it. Mercedes's breath came quick, her body pliant in my grip, her mouth hungry for whatever I gave. I pressed my palm to her cheek, then to her mouth, feeling the hotness of her tongue as she sucked the blood from my thumb. My heart pounded—a wild, desperate rhythm—and I allowed myself to drift, letting the pleasure, the pain, and the memory of fire consume me.

The next bolt of lightning struck so close to the cathedral that the entire room convulsed. In the silence that followed, there was a sound: the guttering of a candle on the desk, the faint hiss as it flickered and died. I looked over Mercedes's head, expecting to see a snuffed wick, but instead there was smoke—a thin, unnatural ribbon of it—curling from the candle as if it were alive.

The smoke drifted toward the ceiling and spread, a trick of the draft... except there was no draft. The window was sealed, the air stagnant and thick, but the smoke proceeded, slow and deliberate, winding in curlicues above the candle's flame before trailing across the width of the room, toward the ceiling, toward me. Toward *us*. My pulse jumped, and for a moment, I was paralyzed… as if the smoke itself pinned me in place.

Mercedes broke the spell. She shifted on her knees, hands braced on my thighs, her breath hot and wet as she pressed her cheek to the inside of my leg. I looked down, and for a split second, the sight of her—mouth open, lips bruised, eyes wide and glassy—was a perfect overlay for the vision in my mind: The Embermage, kneeling, her own mouth parted, her eyes both a challenge and a promise. The lavender scarf flashed at the edge of my vision, and I lost any remaining tether to restraint.

Gripping Mercedes by the jaw, my thumb pressing hard into the hinge of her mouth, I forced her head back. "Stand up and keep your eyes open," I said, and it wasn't a request. She obeyed, her gaze locked on mine, but she waited for something more. Some command, some violence, some permission to be ruined.

I gave it to her.

Shoving her skirt higher, I exposed her, and with a motion that was more animalistic than human, spread her legs and knelt between them, ignoring the cold stone biting my knees. She gasped, the sound raw and primal, but I didn't let her speak. I pressed my mouth to her wetness, my tongue relentless and cruel, grinding her to the edge with every stroke.

She tried to twist away, but I gripped her hips, fingers digging deep, holding her in place as if she might vanish if I loosened my grip. Her taste was sharp, briny, and tinged with my own blood. I devoured her, not for her pleasure nor mine, but to drown out the memory of The Embermage

She came fast—a quiver, a shudder, a desperate whine muffled by her own fist jammed between her teeth.

I didn't stop.

Pressing my tongue deeper, I guided her through the aftershocks, my hands locked cruelly on her hips to keep her from squirming away. Mercedes's legs clamped around my head, thighs shaking, her body seized with violence. Above us, the smoke continued its slow, predatory climb along the ceiling, thickening with every ragged breath she took, every pulse of her racing heart. I watched out of the corner of my eye, consumed by the certainty that the smoke watched me in return.

Mercedes's next orgasm was worse: a drawn-out, punishing thing that left her sobbing into her arm, her fingers clawing at the stone. I took her apart with methodical cruelty, refusing her even a moment to recover. I wanted her wrung out, emptied of all the composure she ever used as a weapon against me. I wanted her so lost in sensation she would forget her own name, let alone the risk, the shame, the sin of it all. Maybe then I could forget as well.

But the smoke wouldn't let me.

I forced Mercedes through yet another orgasm, then another,

until her body trembled so violently I thought she might be seized by demons. Her voice, when it came, was thin and hoarse: "Claude— stop—" but I ignored it, certain she was only playing, testing the limits as she always did. She knew the word to make it truly stop, and thus far, hadn't uttered it. So I pressed her until she was limp, until her knees buckled, until her entire body sagged against mine, her breath coming in shudders that bordered on sobs.

She said it again, but I was lost in the rhythm, in the memory of that scarf and the fever of my own hands. The next time, it was not my name she whispered, but *that* word, the one we agreed on years ago, back when we still believed we could control ourselves around each other. "Sanctuary." It was barely audible, but it stopped me cold.

The world shuddered back into focus: the cold stone, the taste of blood and salt, the rolling thunder echoing through the cathedral. Mercedes's body was slack, her breathing ragged, her face buried in the crook of her arm. I let go, stumbling back and to my feet, every nerve in my body ringing. The air was thick with the scent of sweat and smoke and something sour: panic rising from the pit of my stomach as I took in the wreckage I made of her. Mercedes curled against the base of the window, skirt gathered at her waist, shoulders hunched as if bracing for a blow. I reached for her, hands shaking, but she flinched away—not out of fear, but with the careful, shamed recoil of someone who trusted too much and regretted it instantly.

"Mercedes," I managed, my voice hoarse. "I'm—I'm sorry, I—"

She shook her head, not meeting my eyes. "No. I asked for it." Her voice was raw, the edges dulled with exhaustion and something

I couldn't name. "I always do."

"You did," I agreed carefully, "but that was a lot. Please, let me help you." I knelt beside her, awkward and clumsy, searching her face for a wound I could dress or a mark I could erase. She wiped her mouth with the back of her hand, then pulled her skirt down, gathering herself the same way she always had after our worst moments.

I reached for her again, and she let my hand rest on her shoulder, her skin blazing like a furnace. She trembled, and I hated myself for the tremor in my own hand as I squeezed. Mercedes let it linger for a heartbeat, then shrugged me off, her walls locking back into place with a practiced, brittle snap. I recognized it because it was the same mask I so often wore.

"I should go," Mercedes said, and I didn't know if the moisture in her lashes was rain, sweat, or something else neither of us would name. She gathered her shawl, not bothering to fix her hair, not bothering to meet my eyes. Her skirt was still askew, and I reached to help her, but the look she shot me—flat and exhausted—stopped me cold. "Please, don't."

Guilt gnawed at me as I took in the sight of what I'd made of her. "You need aftercare," I insisted, but remained frozen in place, not wanting to scare her any more than I already had. "Let me dress you, bathe you. Let me walk—" I protested, but Mercedes was already at the door, shoulders squared, back straight.

She paused, hand on the bolt, and for a moment I thought she would say something that would crack us both open. Instead, Mercedes glanced at the desk, at the small wooden bird, and then at me.

"You know," she said, "if you keep feeding that hunger with pain, someday it'll eat you alive." Her words were gentle, but the verdict was final. She opened the door and was gone before I could even stand.

I sat there for a long time, numb and buzzing, the taste of her still sharp on my tongue, the memory of her heat already fading. The storm raged outside, but in the hush that followed Mercedes's departure, I heard only the frantic thud of my own heart. The candle on the desk sputtered and died, the last of its wax pooling around the base, the smoke twining upward like a question I couldn't answer.

Pulling myself to my feet, I braced against the edge of the desk. The room looked no different than it did an hour before, but I felt changed, somehow. Hollowed out, like there was nothing left but the sticky residue of want and regret. The carving of the bird stared at me, its wings spread as if a plea to escape.

I hated myself for what I'd done to Mercedes. For what I became. For the knowledge that, even in the throes of pleasure, the only thing I wanted was the impossible: The Embermage. Not the fantasy, but her raw, unfiltered presence. I wanted her to burn, and I wanted to be her match.

Slumping into my chair, head in my hands, I tried to gather any remaining fragments of resolve. Father Laurent's letter still peeked out from under the ledger, an accusation and a warning both. I couldn't keep this up. I couldn't keep feeding the hunger with pain, or with borrowed bodies, or with the relentless grind of my own guilt. It wasn't working. It would never work. The more I tried to cauterize the desire, the more it gnawed at me, insatiable and wild.

I knew what I had to do.

If I were to have any hope of eradicating my obsession, I would have to face it. Not in fantasy, not in the trembling aftermath of sin, but in the flesh. I would go to her. To see The Embermage, not as a shadow or a fever dream, but as herself. I would stand before her, let her look at me, *truly* look, and allow the horror of my own longing to burn itself out. It would be my final penance.

If I survived, perhaps I would finally be free.

VI. THE STAGE

Esmeralda

The fucking rain was going to ruin everything.

What started as a misting nuisance was now a full-on torrent, dumping sheets of water on the city and flattening even the most stubborn of market awnings. My modest stage had a roof, but not one designed for heavy weather. Already, its boards were slick and treacherous. The crowd clustered under the little shelter they could find, their voices a chorus of complaints. I stood backstage, peeking through a small peephole, scarf clutched to my chest. For the first time in years, I considered canceling.

But I couldn't. Not tonight.

Jules hovered at my elbow, sparks crackling up their arm as they struggled to keep control of their own element. "You'll slip," they hissed, voice sharp with anxiety. "You'll be pac—"

"I know how my own fucking magic works, Jules," I hissed back, harsher than intended, but didn't bother to apologize. The last thing I needed was my sibling lecturing me about pacifiers, the natural opposite of each mage's element, and the one thing that could temporarily extinguish their magic. For fire mages, that was water. I could handle a little rain, but if I got too wet, my flames would go dormant until I was able to dry off.

That wouldn't do.

In my hands, the scarf grew heavier by the second, its beads a cold weight that threatened to drag me under. My second show with it, the first time I intended to *use* it to lure in my prey as I'd intended all along, and the weather was determined to fuck me. I pictured how the scarf might look once it inevitably got soaked. Less a ribbon of fire, more a sodden rag clinging to my skin. Not seductive, simply pathetic. I'd have to burn brighter and hotter just to keep it from turning into a useless scrap of fabric dragging me down.

But if I was being honest, it wasn't the prospect of a drenched finale that made my hands sweat and my stomach roil. It was tonight, and the knowledge that *this* performance had to be perfect. I needed the crowd. I needed the silver-haired man, to ensnare him completely.

Scanning the square through the peephole proved fruitless. The rain turned faces into a blur of hoods and umbrellas. If the silver-haired man was here, he was well hidden. Bitter disappointment lingered on my tongue. The scarf's beads pressed cold and sharp against my palms, and I gripped them, hoping it might stop my hands from quivering. I hoped even more that Jules wouldn't see.

"Es." My sibling's voice came softer now. "Are you sure about this?"

I didn't look at them—I couldn't. "About what, exactly?"

"Why are you so obsessed with him, of all people?"

I wanted to laugh, but it came out as a sigh. "I'm not obsessed. Just focused."

Jules stayed silent, but I refused to turn. Pressing my eye to the peephole again, I ignored the ache in my jaw as I clenched it. The crowd had grown, and the square was now packed despite the storm. It was a sea of umbrellas and cloaks, with every inch of covered space claimed by bodies desperate for distraction or warmth. The sight should have steadied me, but all I could think about was how many eyes would be on me if I slipped. How many would see me fail.

I swept the crowd for that flash of silver hair, that familiar shape. *Nothing.* Disappointment settled in my gut, heavier than the scarf. I built this night around the certainty of his presence, around my carefully-laid trap being executed perfectly, and he wasn't even here. I wanted to set the entire stage ablaze and let the wind carry the cinders to the cathedral, but instead I made myself breathe, slow and even.

Behind me, Jules fidgeted. "You can still call it off," they whispered, their hand hovering near my shoulder but not quite touching. Perhaps they were scared to shock me, or perhaps they were scared of *me.* "No one would blame you."

I turned away from the curtain to face my sibling for the first time. "I'm fine. I can do this."

They didn't look convinced. "Just… don't let them get to you, okay? Not the crowd, not him, not the guards." Their jaw trembled for a second, then steadied. "You're not alone out there, Es."

It was meant to be comforting, but it landed like a threat. There were at least two guards in the front row, their helmets glinting off the street lamps. More waited at the perimeter, hands resting on their weapons, watching the stage with a predatory patience. I wondered if they recognized me, if they saw through the rouge and the paint to the girl whose mother they dragged away. Maybe they did. Maybe that was the real reason I was here—to give them a face to hate, to remind them that we were still standing, still burning, no matter how many families they erased.

I closed my eyes, summoning the memory of Maman's voice: *Never let them see you afraid.* I straightened my spine, let my breath settle, and forced every muscle in my face to relax into a smile. The Embermage would not falter. Not for rain, not for guards, not for the Church, and certainly not for the man who couldn't even be bothered to show up.

The announcer's bell rang once, twice. The crowd shuffled, restless as the rain picked up, a hard patter now, drumming on the boards overhead. I was supposed to be onstage already, halfway through my opening act, but I refused to step out until I saw him. The silver-haired ghost had haunted every performance for months, and now, when I needed him most, he was gone. *Typical.*

I paced the cramped space behind the curtain, scarf wound tight around my wrist, fingertips itching with heat I couldn't quite summon. Jules followed me with their eyes, arms folded tight across their chest, lips pressed in a flat line.

"Are you going to make them wait all night?"

"If I have to," I shot back. "He's always early. Always."

Jules shook their head. "Maybe he's got better things to do than watch you set yourself on fire for a crowd who's seen it a hundred times before."

I flinched, but let the jab slide off me. "He'll come."

The bell rang again, more insistent. A smatter of *boos* rose from the crowd, muffled by the rain. I gritted my teeth and pressed my forehead to the damp wood of the backstage pillar, letting the cold bite through the sweat beading on my skin. The urge to bolt out the back into the alleys, to never look over my shoulder was overwhelming. I focused instead on my pre-show rituals: tighten my boots, smooth my skirt, then the scarf. It was looped three times around my neck and knotted so the beads rested at the hollow of my throat like a string of curses. My hands went through the motions, but my mind scoured the mass of onlookers for the impossible: a flash of silver, the lopsided set of his shoulders, a look that could turn my blood to glass.

Still nothing.

The bell clanged once more, and the crowd's restlessness boiled over. "Bring her out!" someone shouted. "We're freezing out here!" Laughter, then a crack of thunder so close it set the boards vibrating beneath my boots. I jerked back, heart racing, and nearly clocked Jules in the face as I spun.

"I can't do it," I whispered, the words scraping my throat raw.

"He's not here."

Jules grabbed my wrist and squeezed. "Es. Look at me."

I met their gaze, though it took everything I had. Their eyes were so much like Maman's in these moments. Wide and unblinking, as if desperate to keep me alive by force of will alone.

"You're not doing this for him," Jules said, voice low and urgent. "You're doing it for you, for all of us. Don't let some some fucking Church rat make you forget that."

I wanted to believe them, wanted to believe I truly was more than I felt. But the ache in my chest said otherwise. I was so tired of being seen only for the mask I wore onstage, so tired of the loneliness that came after the applause faded. I craved the silver-haired man, and I needed him to desire me back if only to prove I was real.

The crowd's agitation reached a fever pitch. Someone pounded on the makeshift stage, close enough to rattle the curtain. "If you're scared, just say so!" a woman jeered, her words slurred. "We'll find a real mage!" A chorus of laughter followed, brutal and sharp.

Jules's grip only tightened. "Es. You go out there, and you burn like you always do. If he's not there, you burn for *us*."

I nodded, or tried to. The motion was more like a convulsion, my whole body shuddering as I peeled myself off the pillar. I was hollow, a candle burned to the nub. I fixed the scarf in place, let the fabric settle around my shoulders, and took three breaths.

Then I pushed through the curtain.

The noise struck me first: the roar of a crowd too wet and too drunk to care if I lived or died, so long as I gave them a show.

The lights were dimmer than usual, torches struggling against the downpour, shadows flickering up the walls in broken patterns. I could barely see the front row, let alone the faces beyond. *Good.* I didn't want to see them. I wanted to be a force of nature, something the city would remember even as the rain washed me away.

I strutted to center stage, boots squelching with every step, and let the silence stretch, just long enough to make them ache for it. When I raised my hands, the fire came.

It sputtered at first, barely a flicker, then it flared, a heat so sudden it turned the raindrops to steam in a halo around my hands. The crowd gasped, a collective inhalation that nearly drowned out the rain. I let the fire die out before conjuring it again, brighter and hotter, until it danced along my fingertips in a perfect, impossible arc. The scarf caught the glow and magnified it, beads throwing wild sparks across the stage, the violet shimmer alive with every flick of my wrist. I spun, letting the fabric trail behind me, and the fire followed, painting the air with ribbons of gold and blue.

I was The Embermage, everything they wanted me to be. I burned for them, and they roared their approval.

But every time I swept the crowd, searching for the only pair of eyes I cared about, there was nothing but strangers and shadows. I performed every trick I knew, pushed my magic to the edge of depletion, and still, he never came. The absence was physical, a void I couldn't fill. My movements grew sharper, more desperate, the scarf snapping through the air like a whip, beads ringing together in a frantic, discordant music.

I imagined it was his throat I wrapped the silk around, his body twisted and bent to my will. I conjured a vision of him at my feet, hands bound behind his back, mouth open in shock or awe or both. I pictured his eyes, the way they would look up at me as I wove the scarf around his throat and forced him to breathe me in, to taste the smoke and sweat—and lust. The fantasy was so vivid it undid me. My knees trembled, my magic flickered, and for a horrible second I thought I lost the thread.

But the crowd only howled louder, their hunger feeding mine, and I let the image sharpen, let it burn through every fiber of my being. I imagined him begging, not with words but with the arch of his neck, the tremor in his hands, the way his breath would catch as I pressed my heel to his chest and made him watch, made him see what he drove me to do. I wanted him in tatters, gasping and helpless, the mask of his holiness peeled away until there was nothing left but the raw, desperate animal beneath. I wanted to see him break, and I wanted to be the one to hold the pieces.

The scarf was a leash, a chain, a promise. I whipped it through the air, letting the beads catch the light. The crowd shuddered in unison, their faces lit in the afterglow. I wished the thunder of their applause could fill the hollow in my chest as it once had, but it only echoed, louder and emptier each time. Every sweep of the scarf, every crackle of heat, every moment I forced the world to look at me, none of it mattered if he wasn't there. If he didn't see me.

Rain fell with reckless abandon now, a savage onslaught that battered the front of the stage and sent icy rivers down my back as water seeped through the flimsy roof. The torches hissed, their flames shrinking to tiny embers. My magic stuttered, recoiling from the wetness, the fire in my veins foundering as the cold soaked through my sleeves and under my skin. The scarf clung to me, sodden and heavy, beads dragging at my neck like a chain of regret. For a moment, I thought I might collapse, right there in front of everyone—to allow the water douse me, to let the crowd jeer, to watch as the guards dragged my limp body off the boards. It would be better than the humiliation of admitting I came here for nothing.

But I was The Embermage. I was the flame, and I wouldn't be snuffed out by a little rain.

In the faces closest to the stage, there were the beginnings of pity. The guards at the front row snickered to each other, their eyes glittering with the sick pleasure of watching a mage fail. I thought of Maman, of the way she faced her accusers with her head held high, even as they dragged her out by her hair. I thought of Jules, of the Sirots, and of every other name that had been erased from this city by men who smiled as they did it. The urge to explode, to incinerate the whole square, was so strong it made my vision swim.

But the rain wouldn't let me. Not tonight.

I took a step forward, and my foot slid on the slick boards. I barely caught myself, the scarf whipping out as a counterweight, beads flashing like warning bells. Someone in the second row barked a laugh. The guards exchanged a look, and I saw it for what it was: hunger. Not for the show, but for the moment I'd finally fail. The city was full of men who lived for it—the first crack in the mask, the first stumble of flame, the first sign that I was only human after all.

I could have ended it there. Bowed, let the curtain fall, admitted defeat. But I didn't. I stood, knees shaking, and let the silence build. The rain battered the roof like a thousand fists, much of it making its way to me. The crowd leaned in, waiting for the collapse. *My* collapse.

That was when I saw him.

The crowd rippled, bodies shifting to part the way for a hooded figure: tall, broad-shouldered, the set of his jaw unmistakable even from thirty feet away. He pushed through the crowd without ceremony, weaving through the masses, not stopping until he stood at the very edge of the stage, face upturned, water streaming off the peak of his brow. In the lamplight his eyes shone black, but I knew them well enough to see the blue even in the storm. The sight of him, real and present and near, hit me harder than any blow. I stared, breathless, as the world narrowed to the space between us.

He was soaked. Cloak plastered to his body, hair slicked back to reveal the sharp angles of his face. The rain washed away whatever mask he might have worn, and I saw him as he was: tired, haunted, and so beautiful it made my chest ache. He didn't smile. He didn't flinch. He just stood there, hands at his sides, as if daring me to fail in front of him.

The crowd disappeared. The rain faded. There was only the line that ran from my heart to his, taut as a bowstring. The heat returned, slow and steady, like a stoked coal now flaring to life. Maybe it was his presence, or maybe it was the way he looked at me, as if I was the only thing in the world that mattered.

I felt it before the crowd saw it. The chill of the rain on my skin vanished, replaced by a fierce warmth that radiated from my core, turning the water to steam on my sleeves and in my hair. The sodden scarf began to dry, its violet hue deepening as the heat rose from my skin. The two sputtering torches on either side of the stage didn't just relight—they erupted, flames leaping twice as high as before, their heat so intense that the front row of the crowd flinched back with a collective gasp.

I lifted my hands, and this time, the fire came not as a flicker but a torrent. It poured from my palms, a solid sheet of gold and crimson that defied the downpour, the rain hissing and evaporating a foot from my skin. The snickering guards were silent now, their faces pale in the sudden, violent light.

My performance was no longer just cheap entertainment. It was a declaration of war. I met the silver-haired man's gaze from across the stage, fully aware this was the closest we'd ever been. I let the scarf unfurl, now light and alive again, and whipped it through the air. A shower of sparks, bright as stars, rained down on the wet boards between us. He didn't move, didn't flinch. He just watched, his expression unreadable.

I smiled. Not the practiced grin of The Embermage, but a slow, dangerous curve of the lips that was all my own.

It was a promise. It was a threat.

It was only for him.

VII. THE PERFORMANCE

Claude

I ran as if possessed, and Quasimodo could barely keep up. The streets blurred around me, my boots pounding on the cobblestone with a brutality that was both foreign and inevitable. Behind me came Quasimodo's pleas for me to slow down, his endless questions about what was wrong or whether he was in trouble, but I couldn't bring myself to answer them, much less acknowledge him. He was with me only because I couldn't bear to lie to him yet again. I kept running, each step reckless, every turn a near-miss with some staggering drunk or huddled beggar. Bells tolled the hour behind me, distorted by the rain into a single raw scream.

I kept my head down, hood pulled tight, the city narrowed

to a single task: reach the market, find her, let the fire cauterize whatever sickness was devouring me from the inside out, and be done with it—forever. Whether I meant to confront her or whatever demon lived on inside me, or if I could even tell the difference, I no longer knew.

My hands ached with the memory of violence. Mercedes's voice echoed in my skull: if *you keep feeding that hunger with pain, someday it'll eat you alive.* I wondered if she knew that I was already consumed.

The city fell away, the Seine dividing Paris like a wound, and I found myself at the gates of the mages' market, the night alive with the restless hum of rain and anticipation. Lanterns bobbed above the awnings, casting long shadows over the crowd. The square was choked with bodies despite the weather, a mass of slick cloaks and uplifted faces, all drawn to the makeshift stage at its center. The Embermage's crowd. Her flock. My heresy.

Quasimodo pushed past me, any amount of ire he had toward me forgotten as he ran toward the stage, pushing through the crowd, seemingly headed for the front row. I should have gone after him, should have kept him within arm's reach. But I could do nothing but brace for the sight of her, for her mere presence to strike a match to my nerves, but when I forced my own way through the masses, following Quasimodo's path—a shoulder here, a muttered curse there—what I saw was not the inferno of my memory.

She was failing.

It was unthinkable. The Embermage, who always appeared untouchable, inhuman, a god in her own right, looked smaller than I'd ever seen. Her hair hung limp with rain. Her arms trembled as she raised them, flame sputtering from her palms and dying just as quickly, a pathetic display that left the crowd restless and unimpressed.

She wore the same violet scarf that haunted my dreams and nightmares alike, but the soaked fabric clung to her throat, beads of water strung along its length like tears. The effect was less a mage and more a martyr, and the sight of it stabbed at something deep, something I had not permitted myself to feel since the night I watched my mother die.

It nearly broke me. I braced for seduction, for spectacle, for the cruel pleasure of being seen and destroyed by her in equal measure. I had not expected frailty, for the shivering woman drowning before my eyes. The crowd turned on her. I could feel it in the restless churn, the way their hunger soured from disappointment, to that old, ugly eagerness. The guards at the edge of the stage sniggered, their hands slack on their weapons.

A woman in the front row called out, "Come now, Embermage! Can't take a little rain?" The laughter that followed was hard, pitiless. I recognized it because it was the only music my own childhood had ever known.

I pushed closer, not caring who I shoved aside. The Embermage gathered herself at the lip of the stage, chest heaving. She tried to conjure her fire again, but it flickered and died, the light barely reaching her fingertips before the next wave of rain snuffed it out. I saw, in the flex of her jaw, the near certainty that she was about to snap.

The crowd, eager for her ruin, pressed closer.

I'd never seen her like this, not even in my most desperate fantasies. The Embermage, undone. Her features blurred by water and shame, her power leaking away before an audience ready to devour her. The memory of my own humiliation flared so hot and fast I nearly turned and ran. Instead, I found myself moving forward, drawn by a force that was as much compulsion as it was compassion. I came here to be consumed, to let her destroy me once and for all. I had not imagined I might instead *save* her.

The guards were the first to notice my approach. They bristled, faces hardening to stone. I kept my head down, hoping the cloak and the darkness would suffice, but their suspicion chewed holes in my disguise with every step. Still, I forced my way to the front, stopping only when I stood at the edge of the stage, within reach of her boots. The rain was louder here, the heat of the torches searing my cheeks and making my breath hiss in my ears.

I looked up, and for the first time, The Embermage looked down.

She saw me. No—she *found* me, out of a hundred faces, as if she knew all along where I would be. Her eyes were not the bright green I remembered, but dull and feral, flooded with fear and something that might have been hope. For a moment, nothing happened. The world fell silent in that split-second, perfectly suspended in stillness.

Her jaw set. Her back straightened. The trembling in her arms stilled, replaced by a slow, deliberate grace that sent a shiver through the crowd. She didn't smile. She didn't wink or acknowledge the jeers of the market. She simply raised her hands, and with a snap of her wrist, the soaked scarf unwound from her throat and coiled around her fingers as if it were alive.

The crowd stopped, sudden and absolute.

She began to dance.

Not like before. None of the practiced flourishes or showy tricks I saw week after week, but something raw and desperate, stripped of performance. She moved as if the stage were a battlefield, as if every step measured against some invisible enemy. The scarf, heavy with rain, defied gravity. I forgot the rest of the world existed as the market, the rain, even the guards faded to static. The only real thing was *her*.

Her body carving a path through the air, her hands weaving the scarf into new shapes with each movement. She wielded it both like a weapon and an old lover, sometimes snapping it through the empty space above my head, sometimes letting it graze her cheek as if it were the only comfort she had ever known. The beads clicked together, a counterpoint to the drum of rain and my own heartbeat roaring in my ears.

She circled the stage, never once breaking her gaze from mine. There was no seduction now, only the pure, brutal fact of her will: that she would not be ruined, not tonight, not for them. The scarf, drenched as it was, became an extension of her, a thread that tethered her to the world of the living even as her magic flickered at the edge of exhaustion.

I was shaking, and hadn't felt so powerless since the day I'd been pressed to the cold stone floor of the Abbey, Laurent's hand in my hair, the taste of blood and incense thick in my mouth. The world was spinning, and the only thing that anchored me was the impossible fact that she was alive and burning, refusing to let herself be extinguished.

The Embermage danced as if there were no one else, not the crowd, not the guards, not Quasimodo, not even God. Only me, her, and the scarf that bound us together. The movements were reckless, almost ugly in their honesty. Her hair plastered flat to her skull, her chest yanking with the effort of each step. The water on her skin steamed as she spun, droplets vaporizing in the heat that poured from her even in exhaustion. The scarf whipped through the air, a violet blur, and as she drew closer toward me warmth radiated from her, hot enough to dry the rain from my own face. I was so near I could make out each bead on the scarf, glistening with a different color.

She snapped the scarf forward, the end of it cracking the air a finger's width above my head. The crowd gasped, but I didn't flinch. Her eyes remained fixed on me, measuring my reaction. I let her see that I would not be moved—not by the rain, not by the crowd, not by her. If she wanted to break me, to shatter the mask I so carefully wore, she would have to try harder.

And she did.

The dance changed. Her movements grew sharper, more violent, as if locked in combat with something only she could see. The scarf lashed the air, leaving afterimages of purple and blue that burned into my vision. Each time she spun, the fire flared brighter, the heat of it pushing back the cold and the damp. I felt it in my teeth, in my bones, in the soft curve of my throat where the scarf might one day rest. She was no longer performing for the crowd. She performed for me, for whatever darkness we shared.

It was unbearable. The intimacy of it, the focus, the way she made the rest of the world disappear until I was the only witness to her ruin or her triumph. I wanted to look away. I wanted to run. Instead, I stood there like a sacrifice, waiting for her to finish what she started.

The crowd sensed the shift. Their jeers faded, replaced by an uneasy hush. To my left, Quasimodo clasped his hands tightly, indicating his anxiety. Even the guards seemed unsure, glancing at each other as if waiting for permission to intervene. But no one dared move. The Embermage took control of the night and was not about to let anyone take it back. The crowd was hers, the city was hers, and for one suspended heartbeat, even I belonged to her.

She stopped dancing.

The silence was total. Even the rain seemed to pause, uncertain what to do with itself. She stood so close to me I could see the rise and fall of her chest, the droplets beading on her lashes, the faint shaking in her hands. The scarf—her weapon, her shield, her only vestige of power—hung limp from her shoulders, no longer slick with rain, as the warmth from her fire had completely dried it out.

Her gaze shifted slightly. It was not the look of a predator, or a lover, or even an enemy. It was the look of someone who had nothing left to lose. My lips parted, a wordless confession on the tip of my tongue, but she moved before I could speak. Kneeling at the edge of the stage, the boards slick and treacherous, she reached for me.

I didn't move. I couldn't.

Her hand brushed my cheek, soft and warm, and she leaned forward until her face was inches from mine. Somewhere behind me came the uneasy shuffle of guards, the crowd's collective breath held tight as a noose.

For a paralyzing instant, the world stilled—each drop of rain suspended in the air, each face in the crowd a frozen mask. She was close enough to kiss, and I was close enough to ruin everything.

There was a glint in her eyes, full of something I couldn't name. Her hand hovered at my cheek, drifting lower, the back of her fingers tracing the line of my jaw. I felt the heat of her, even through the damp fabric of my hood, a promise and a threat both. My own breath was shallow, desperate, as if I never learned to breathe until this moment.

She didn't speak. Instead, she reached up, slow as the turn of the world, and drew the violet scarf from her own neck. The beads caught the light, each one a tiny star trembling on the verge of collapse. I watched, helpless, as she wound the scarf around her hand, then—so deliberate, so gentle—wrapped it once, twice, around my throat.

I flinched. Not from pain, but from the shock of being claimed so openly, so absolutely, in front of my son, the city, the Church, and God Himself.

The scarf was hot from her skin, and settled at my throat with a comforting weight. Her fingers lingered, brushing the edge of my jaw—tender, almost reverent. The world contracted to that point of contact. I was no longer aware of the storm, Quasimodo, the crowd, or the guards at my back. There was only her, and the scent of lilac and smoke that clung to the silk, and the impossible, excruciating fact of her hand at my neck.

She leaned in. For a moment, I believed she might kiss me. I wanted her to. I wanted to close the last inch of space between us, to surrender to the gravity that ruined every good thing in my life, to let her devour me in front of everyone. The hunger was so sharp it bordered on agony.

But she drew back, her gaze never leaving mine, and cinched the scarf tight enough that I felt the beads press into my neck. It was a warning. A gift. A promise, a sentence, and the only absolution I would ever know.

The crowd erupted, the spell broken in a surge of cheers and catcalls, the city's hunger for spectacle sated. Noise battered me from all sides, and the guards behind surged forward, boots splashing with blades at the ready, voices barking over the crowd. The atmosphere shifted from awe to panic in a single instant. I lost sight of Quasimodo, but before I could bolt in the direction I'd last seen him, a hand, foreign and rough, clamped around my shoulder, spinning me away from the stage.

"Enough!" barked the man who touched me, and when I turned, I recognized him: the newly appointed Captain of the Guard, Phoebus. His yellow hair was plastered to his skull, rain streaming down his face. "Show's over. You've had your fun."

The Embermage didn't flinch. She stood at the edge of the stage, hands raised and empty, the fire gone but her eyes brighter than ever. The scarf remained wound around my neck, its warmth seeping into my skin, a brand I would never be rid of. I wanted to reach for her, to pull her from the stage and shield her from the guards, but my arms refused to move. I was transfixed, helpless, every nerve in my body singing with the memory of her touch.

The guards mounted the stage two at a time, with Phoebus the first to reach it. The crowd recoiled, but The Embermage didn't. She watched him approach, her arms crossed, the line of her jaw set. Calculation flickered behind her eyes: fight, flight, or the third thing—whatever had kept her alive this long.

"Pack it up," Phoebus shouted, voice slicing through the faire's chaos. "You're done for the night, unless you want to spend it in a cell." He jerked his chin at his men, who fanned out behind him.

The Embermage shouted something back at him, her lips moving in a defiant snarl, but her words were lost to me, swallowed by the roar of the crowd and the hissing rain. They exchanged a few more quips I couldn't make out, the tension only escalating until The Embermage broke it.

She turned, back arched, and sauntered to the center of the stage. The crowd surged forward, a crush of bodies eager for riot or rescue or both. Phoebus raised a hand to signal his men, but The Embermage was faster. With one fluid motion, she snapped her fingers, and a wall of fire erupted between her and the guards. Phoebus staggered back, cursing, his men scrambling for footing on the wet boards. The crowd screamed, a living wave of fear and excitement, but I stood rooted, the heat searing my face. The flames couldn't last—not in this rain, not with her so spent—but for a glorious instant, the entire stage was a cathedral, and she was its furious, untouchable god.

I almost cheered.

But the fire vanished, and with it the spell. The Embermage swayed, her body clearly spent from pushing her magic to its limits. Phoebus recovered quickly, barking orders, his men swarming the stage. The Embermage looked to me, her eyes full of triumph and terror.

I saw what she meant to do.

"No!" I shouted, voice ripping from my throat before I could think, and lunged. Not forward, but a desperate side-step toward the stage, hands raised as if to ward off a blow not meant for me. The guards surged up the boards in a tangle of boots and elbows, their weapons drawn. I caught the eye of The Embermage, her mouth open in a half-formed shout, her body tensed to run or fight… or both.

Our gazes locked. For another breathless moment, the world shrank to nothing but the two of us, the scarf burning against my throat, her eyes wide with a horror that wasn't fear but recognition. She saw me—saw what I was about to do—and shook her head.

Don't, she mouthed, so clear I easily read her lips over the riot.

I froze, boots rooted in the mud. One of the guards reached for her arm, but she twisted away, the motion so fluid it looked rehearsed.

Two others flanked her, and closed in. Phoebus bellowed something, but it was lost in the chaos. The Embermage backed toward the rear of the stage, seemingly trapping herself further.

Words poured from my throat—a plea, a prayer, and a warning all at once—but there was nothing I could do as the guards converged, ready to drag her off to God-knew-where to do God-knew-what. I couldn't bear it, even less so to watch, but neither could I look away.

And then, with the grace of a saint and the cunning of a devil, The Embermage vanished.

One moment she was there, pressed to the boards, eyes locked on mine; the next, she was gone, swallowed by the stage itself, as if the world opened up to reclaim her. The guards collided where she stood, clawing at empty air and cursing in disbelief. For a heartbeat, the crowd was silent, stunned; then the square erupted in a howl of laughter, derision, and wonder. Phoebus spun on his heel, scanning the shadows for some sign of her, but there was nothing. No flame, no trace, not even a scorch on the wet boards to prove she had ever been there at all.

The loss was like a blow to the chest. At my neck, the scarf went suddenly cold, the memory of The Embermage's touch receding as swiftly as she herself had. I pressed my fingers to the beads, desperate to hold onto the heat, the certainty, the impossible nearness of her. But the world rushed in to fill the void she left behind, the guards barking orders, the crowd surging in every direction, the rain resuming its relentless assault on the city.

I didn't remember leaving the square, and I didn't remember

how I'd located Quasimodo.

One moment, the world was fire and rain and the thundering of my heart. The next, we stumbled through the alley behind the market, lungs heaving, boots skidding on the slick stones. Quasimodo signed frantically into my hand, and muffled chaos echoed behind us—guards shouting, the crowd's delighted, nervous shrieks, the bark of Phoebus echoing off the walls—but it faded with every step, drowned out by the blood in my ears and the ghost of fingers at my throat.

The scarf was there, and it was real. I clutched it in both hands, half-afraid it would vanish if I let go. It was warm again, as if it still carried her pulse, her magic, the last fragment of her will. I pressed it to my lips, then to my cheek, then—ashamed, desperate—shoved it beneath the collar of my cloak, and kept running.

With each step, the silk around my throat grew heavier than any sin I had ever confessed.

VIII. THE GAMBIT

Esmeralda

My entire body quivered as my feet struck the ground. I barely registered the jolt, consumed by giddiness as the trapdoor slammed shut, the shouting silenced, and darkness swallowed me.

I did it.

I *made* it.

Lungs burning, I slumped against the wall, listening to the throb of my pulse echo down the tunnel. For a moment, I did nothing but breathe, the stench of centuries-old stone filling my mouth. Then, as the last scraps of adrenaline seeped out of my muscles, I laughed. Quietly at first, then louder, until the sound bounced back from the dark like applause.

This passageway wasn't large, but it wasn't claustrophobic, either. Water seeped down the walls, pooling at my boots, but I was too tired to care. I ran my hands along the familiar grooves, shuffling forward by muscle memory alone. This was the first trick Maman ever taught me: *Always have an exit. Always know the way out, even if you have to dig it yourself.* I spent half my childhood in these tunnels, learning the city's veins better than my own body. Even when the world above tried to erase us, Paris remembered.

Even in my nearly-depleted state, I could have lit a small flame for comfort or even to help guide me, but didn't. I wanted to relish the dark, let it press in around me, to bear witness to what I'd done. I moved fast, half-running, the flare of each breath a spark in my chest. The further I got from the stage, the less my hands shook, and the less I cared about the bruises blooming on my shins. All of it was proof that I'd not only survived, but outwitted the guards, out-danced the storm, and out-burned the city's hunger for my ruin.

But that wasn't the only thing making my heart race. It was how the silver-haired man looked *into* me when the scarf landed around his throat. The shock, the awe, the desire. I saw a thousand faces in the crowd, but none had ever looked at me as if I were both a savior and a curse. The memory of it came over and over again, enough to make my skin prickle. It was the best kind of high—better than the rush of magic, better than applause, better even than the first trembling gasp of a lover's mouth against mine. I'd done more than survive. I made him see me, *really* see me, and left him haunted by the absence where I'd been.

The tunnel arced left, then right, then spiraled down a few steps, each one slick with moss. I continued to run my fingers along the wall, counting the ridges by touch, letting my mind replay the details on a loop.

I didn't rush the last stretch. I slowed, savoring the anticipation, the way it curled tight in my belly like a secret. At the end of the passage, the brickwork opened into the hollow behind my bedroom wall, and I tumbled out, scraping my knuckles on the stone as I fumbled for the latch. The panel swung open in a hush of dust and cold air, and I all but collapsed into the softness of my own bed, the familiar creak of the frame grounding me in the present. For a moment, I lay there, face buried in the tangled sheets, the smell of sweat, candle wax, and last night's perfume wrapping me up like a cocoon. Every muscle in my body unclenched, the tension leaking out of me until I was a loose, boneless puddle of nerves.

I rolled onto my back, staring at the cracked plaster of the ceiling, and let the afterglow settle over me. The room was quiet— no Jules, no Antoine, no roar of the crowd or the market. Just me, the silence, and the echo of my performance still vibrating in my bones. I pressed my palms to my cheeks, half expecting to find them burning, but the only heat was a slow, delicious simmer that started in my gut and radiated outward, as if the fire inside me had finally found room to breathe.

I laughed again, softer this time, and stretched my arms overhead. Closing my eyes, I savored every detail of what I'd just accomplished: the roar of the crowd, the fire in my hands, the look on the silver-haired man's face when the scarf wound around his throat and he didn't move, didn't flinch, just let himself be claimed in front of everyone. The guards scrambling, the Captain's face gone pale, the rain hissing on the flames, but unable to put them out. The image replayed in my mind, sharper and more vivid with each pass, until I was sure I'd never forget it. I'd done exactly what I set out to do: made him want me, made the city fear me, made them all remember that The Embermage did not go quietly, not for anyone.

My breath slowed as my heart, at last, remembered how to beat. I flexed my fingers, still tingling with magic, and let the sensation run up my arms and into my chest. I was alive, I was whole, and for the first time in months, I didn't feel like I was waiting for the other shoe to drop. I let myself drift, eyes half-closed, until the knots in my spine had all but melted into the mattress. I could have stayed here forever, floating on the memory of tonight.

A sharp knock at the door shattered my reverie. I bolted upright, heart launched in my throat. Then came the second knock. It was more like a code, a tiny stutter between the raps, which could only be Jules. I braced myself for the inevitable.

The door swung inward, and my sibling stood in the doorway, hair still damp from the rain, eyes pinched with worry and something close to rage. They didn't bother to pretend to be relieved I wasn't in prison—or worse. "You could have gotten yourself killed," they spat, voice trembling. "Gotten *us* killed."

"No one died, Jules. Not even close." I groaned and rolled my eyes. "If you're here to lecture me, at least let me get out of these wet clothes first."

Jules ignored me, crossing the room in three quick strides. They grabbed my wrist, hauling me upright so fast my vision whited out. "You're a fucking idiot," they hissed, then hugged me with enough force to knock the breath from my lungs. Surprised, I tried to squirm away, but Jules held on, quivering. "You can't just vanish like that. You can't leave me to clean up your mess every time you want to prove a point."

"I didn't vanish," I protested, but it was half-hearted. I let Jules hold on as long as they needed, because the truth was, I needed it, too. The relief in their voice, the tension in their grip, said more than any lecture could.

They pulled away, their face stormy. "You need to come downstairs. Now. Everyone's waiting." Then, softer: "You're in deep shit, Es."

I rolled my eyes again, but let them pull me out of the room and down the narrow staircase, my bare feet slipping on the warped treads. The kitchen was a furnace of tension—Antoine and Isabella hunched at the table, jaws clenched, mugs cooling in their hands. Henrietta perched on the windowsill, knitting abandoned in her lap, eyes red-rimmed and furious. The air was thick with equal parts anticipation and dread as Jules released me, stepping back, yet notably blocking the hall—my only escape. "There. She's alive. Happy now?"

Henrietta's knitting clattered to the floor as she shot up. "You absolute fool," she said, voice sharp as a slap. "Do you have any idea how close you came—"

"To what?" I interrupted, forcing my own voice to stay steady. "Getting arrested? Killed? Or just embarrassing you all?"

Antoine, arms folded so tight his knuckles went white, cut in. "You nearly incited a full on riot. They sent two patrols to the market. They're searching the alleys as we speak, and the Captain of the Guard is demanding a list of every mage in the district." His glare was sharper than the city guards' blades. "You think you're clever, Esmeralda? You just painted a target on all our backs."

I shrugged, feigning a confidence I didn't feel. "They were always going to come for us. Nothing I did tonight changed that."

Henrietta scoffed. "You don't get it, do you? This new Captain isn't at all like the incompetent old fool we had before. They say Phoebus is a zealot, and he's itching to make an example of someone."

"Let him try," I shot back, too loud. "He's just another dog on a leash, barking wherever he's ordered. They all are."

Jules slammed their palm on the table. "You're missing the point! Every fucking time you pull a stunt like this, you put all of us in danger—me, Henrietta, even the kids who run our errands. You think you're the only one who matters?"

That stung, but I refused to let it show. "I'm the only one doing *anything*. The rest of you are content to hide and hope the world forgets we exist."

Isabella snorted, her eyes narrow and cold. "You're reckless. You're going to get us all killed for a stage trick."

"It wasn't a trick," I snapped, voice sharp as broken glass. "It was a message. I made them watch, I made them remember. For once, we weren't the ones hiding." The words came out hot, and I couldn't stop now, wouldn't even if I wanted to. "You should all be thanking me. I did in one night what the Council hasn't managed in a decade. I made the city afraid of us. I made them respect us."

Antoine scoffed, but Henrietta cut him off, voice wavering. "You think fear is the same thing as respect? You think the Church won't double their patrols, won't start rounding us up—"

"That's exactly what they're already doing!" I shouted. "Or did you forget the Sirots? Or the purge last winter? We're already at war, whether you want to admit it or not. You want to cower and wait for them to erase us, fine. But don't pretend I'm the villain for fighting back."

The room quieted. I could see the pain in Henrietta's eyes, the frustration in Jules's, the flick of resignation in Antoine's. For one dizzying heartbeat, I thought I won, that I forced them into understanding. But then a new voice sliced through the room, low and cold as the Seine in winter:

"Is that what you think your mére died for?"

The rebuke was so sudden and sharp it rang in my ears. I turned, and there he was: Papa, leaning in the threshold, arms folded, the old velvet of his jacket gone threadbare at the elbows. His eyes, always sharp, pinned me to the spot with a precision that made every inch of me want to shrink.

Nobody moved. Nobody breathed. Even the needles Henrietta retrieved from the floor stilled mid-air.

Papa let the silence stretch until it pulled the heat from my cheeks and left me raw. "Well?" he said at last, his voice so quiet it was more of a threat than a question. "Is that what you believe? That she wanted you to turn martyrdom into a spectacle?"

I opened my mouth, but the words tangled in my throat. "I'm not—I didn't—"

"Didn't what?" He stepped into the room, boots barely making a sound on the kitchen tile. "Didn't get yourself killed? Didn't think about what comes *after* the performance?"

The words were a slap, but what stung most was the look in his eyes: not anger, but something worse. Disappointment. Grief. A kind of raw, bottomless fear that made me want to fold up and disappear.

I squared my shoulders, but the heat was already leaking out of me. "I did what I had to do."

Papa shook his head, slow and deliberate. "You did what you *wanted* to do. There's a difference." The room was so still I could make out the tick of the clock over the hearth, and the slow drip of rainwater from the eaves outside.

He moved closer, and the familiar scent of smoke rose from his coat. "You think you're clever. You think you're the only one who ever tried to outsmart them. But you're not." He paused, the weight of his words building. "Your mére thought the same. She thought she could be clever, too. And it cost her everything."

I wanted to argue, to shout, to blame him for all the ways he failed to protect us, but couldn't. All I could do was stare at the floor. Papa's words hung in the air, the finality of them landing as if he slapped me. I looked up, expecting more—an apology, a softening, anything—but there was nothing. Just that hollowed-out gaze, the one he wore at Maman's funeral, the one he'd never taken off since.

"I'm not her," I said, quieter than I meant to. "I'm not trying to—"

He cut me off with a glance. "But you are, Esmeralda. You're making the same mistakes." His jaw worked, as if he was chewing on something bitter. "You want to be a symbol? Symbols get people killed."

I bristled, ready to snap that I'd rather die fighting than live a coward, but Henrietta beat me to it. "Clopin, she's right. We can't keep hiding forever—"

He rounded on her, voice still low but vibrating with anger. "What's your plan, then? Burn the city down? Let them come for us in the night, one by one, until no one's left?" His fists clenched at his sides. "We are not strong enough for open war. Not yet."

"Then when?" I demanded, the old fury rising again. "When we're all gone? When you're the last mage left in the city, cowering behind locked doors and praying the Church forgets you exist?" My voice shook, but I didn't care. "I won tonight. I beat them, Papa. I made them see us, and all you can do is scold me like I'm still a child."

He didn't flinch. He didn't even blink. "You think this is a victory?" he said, voice so cold it burned. "A victory is when our people are safe, but right now, that safety is only because they're damn greedy. The only reason Captain Phoebus and his men aren't kicking down every door on this street right now is because I had to empty the Council's emergency coffers to pay him off. A *bribe*, Esmeralda. That's your victory."

Jules let out a sharp, indrawn breath. Henrietta looked down at her hands.

"That money," Papa continued, his voice dangerously quiet, "was for the Widows' and Orphans' Fund. It was meant to help the Sirots' children, if we could find them. It was for the next family the Church decides to erase. Now it's gone, lining the pockets of the very men who hunt us, all to clean up the mess from your… performance. Not that it would have mattered in this case, though."

For the barest second, he looked away, as if he wanted to swallow the words. But he forced them out, each one a nail in my chest.

"The Sirots are dead, Esmeralda. They found them this morning. All of them."

All of them. The words landed with such forcefulness I missed the rest. My mouth opened, but nothing came out. Henrietta gasped, her hands flying to her face. Jules made a choking sound, a wordless protest that curdled into a sob. Antoine stared at his mug, jaw clenched so tight his teeth might shatter, while Isabelle threw herself into his shoulder as she cried.

"You're lying," I said once I was able to form words, but even as they left my lips, I knew how hollow they sounded. The Sirots had been ghosts since the last sweep, their stall at the market untouched, the little girl's toys left scattered on the stone as if she might come back for them. I knew, but refused to believe, despite having seen their ransacked house with my own eyes.

Papa's gaze didn't waver. "You want to save us, Esmeralda? Then stop making yourself the excuse they need to kill us all."

I wanted to scream. I wanted to punch the wall, or him, or every brittle, frightened face in the room. Instead, I just stood there, the weight of my own arrogance pinning me in place. I had no words left. None that mattered.

So I bolted—out of the kitchen, up the stairs, into the dark of my room—slamming the door so hard the latch splintered. I pressed my back to it, breathing in quick, shallow bursts as my pulse hammered at the base of my skull. The world outside had become muffled, as if the storm knew to quiet just for me. I sank to the floor, knees pulled tight, and tried not to picture the Sirots.

It was a mistake. Some bureaucratic fuckup, some cruel rumor. Maybe the Sirots had run, perhaps they managed to slip away before the Captain sniffed them out. But I saw the look in Papa's eyes. It was the same look from the night he told me Maman wasn't coming home. That expression didn't lie.

A soft knock came at the door, so quiet I almost thought I'd imagined it. I didn't answer. The door creaked open anyway, and Jules stood in the threshold. Their anger was gone, replaced by something hollowed out and fragile. They took in the sight of me curled on the floor, and the last of their fight seemed to leave them in a single, ragged exhale.

They closed the door and slid down to the floor across from me, their knees drawn up just like mine. We sat in silence for a long moment, the chasm of our argument still between us.

"I shouldn't have said what I said," Jules whispered finally, their voice raw. "About Maman. That wasn't fair."

I just shook my head, unable to speak.

"But Papa's right," they continued, their own voice breaking on a sob they tried to swallow. "You're just like her. So brave, and so stubborn, and so stupidly reckless. I... I watched them take her, Esme. I can't... I can't watch them take you, too."

Tears streamed down their face now, hot and silent. The sight of them, so completely undone, shattered the last of my own hardened rage. I crawled across the floor and wrapped my arms around them, and we clung to each other, two halves of the same grief.

"I won't let them," I murmured into their hair, the words a lie I wanted desperately to believe.

Jules pulled back, their hands gripping my arms, their eyes fierce and pleading. "Then promise me," they said, their voice urgent. "Promise me you'll stop. That man, your plan, whatever it is... it's not worth it. Let it go. Swear to me, Esme. Swear on Maman's grave that you will let him go."

The oath hung in the air between us, the most sacred one we had. To swear on her was a vow that couldn't be broken. I saw the cost of refusal in Jules's eyes—a future of sleepless nights and constant terror, waiting for the knock on the door that would take me away, too. The rage I felt for the Sirots, the hunger I felt for the silver-haired man... none of it felt worth the pain I was causing my sibling in this moment.

The fight went out of me. The word was a betrayal of the cold resolve still forming in my gut, but looking at Jules's face, I said it anyway. My voice was a ghost.

"I promise."

Jules collapsed against me, their relief so absolute it was like a physical weight. We stayed like that for a long time, until their breathing evened out. When they finally pulled away, they gave me a watery, exhausted smile, kissed my forehead, and left without another word, closing the door softly behind them.

I sat alone in the quiet, the promise I'd just made already feeling like ash in my mouth. Jules believed me. They would sleep tonight, believing their sister was safe, that the danger had passed. But as I dragged myself to my feet and walked to the window, my gaze finding the distant, dark spires of Notre Dame, I knew the truth.

The Sirots were still dead. The man with silver hair was still out there.

And a promise, weighed against the memory of a ghost, was not enough to stop what had to be done.

Pressing my palms to my face, I tried to clear the image in my mind's eye. Instead, I saw the scarf and the silver-haired man's ruined, beautiful face as I wound it around his throat. The way he looked at me, the hunger and the helplessness, how his hands shook as if he already knew what I'd done. The memory twisted inside me, cold and sharp as a blade.

Had it been him? The thought came so fast and so ugly I almost choked on it. Had the silver-haired man—my obsession, my mark—been the one to give the order, or worse, to carry it out himself?

Forcing myself to envision it, I tried to picture him standing in the Sirots' parlor, hands folded and eyes cold, watching as the guards tore the place apart. I tried to picture him giving the signal, nodding once, then turning away as if it were nothing. I tried to imagine him indifferent, or cruel, or even… complicit.

But I couldn't. Not really. Not even when the next thought that followed, quick and brutal, came to the fore: if he was, it only made me want to ruin him even more.

I hated myself for it. I hated every twisted, selfish inch of my own hunger. How the ache at the pit of my stomach only deepened, how I could still feel his heart hammering under my palm, the silk of the scarf hot between us. The world might be crumbling, my family might be right, but I didn't care. I wanted to see him again. I wanted to look him in the eye and make him flinch, make him remember, make him burn for me the way I burned for him.

The thought didn't comfort me, but it did settle something inside. I wasn't going to apologize. Not to my father, not to Jules, not to anyone. I made my play. Now I just had to wait for the city, for the guard, for the Church, and for the silver-haired man himself to make theirs.

The storm outside thinned to a mist, the city's lights blurring gold and blue through my window. I dragged myself upright and leaned on the sill, pressing my forehead to the glass. Paris after rain was a different beast: softer, the sharp edges dulled, as if the whole world were caught in the moment between breaths. I watched water trickle down to the market square, where the makeshift stage still stood—a waterlogged altar to my own recklessness.

Far beyond, across the sweep of rooftops and the river's slow curve, loomed Notre Dame Cathedral. No lights in the high windows, no silhouette lining the towers, but I could feel eyes watching me even from here. I wondered if he was inside, alone, pacing the length of some holy corridor and tasting the memory of my hand at his throat. I wondered if he kept the scarf, if he pressed it to his mouth and breathed me in, if he cursed my name in the lull between prayers.

I pressed my fingertips to the glass and traced the crooked spire, the jagged line of the roof where lightning struck last year—a jagged, blackened scar that refused to heal. The city was full of scars like that, and the silver-haired man was, too. I saw as much in his eyes, in the moment after the scarf slipped from my neck—how he touched it, almost reverently, how he looked at me like I was the only real thing in the world. Even now, the memory made my skin bristle, a shiver that started at the base of my spine and radiated outwards. It was a hunger, yes, but it was also a promise. I showed him my power, and he had not looked away. He had not run. He let me claim him in front of God and everyone.

That wasn't the act of a coward, or a zealot, or even a true believer. That was the act of someone who understood the rules of the game and was willing to play anyway.

Pulling away from the window, I began to strip, removing each layer as reverently as I wished the silver-haired man would. Bruises dotted my skin—some from the guards, but most from the passion with which I flung myself all over that stage mere hours earlier. As I slipped between my still-warm sheets, it dawned on me that I no longer cared what Papa or Jules or any of the others thought. Let them call me reckless. Let them think me mad. I knew what I was doing, just as Maman had: the only way to win was to risk everything, just as I had tonight.

The pieces were set. My move had been made.

The only thing to do now was wait.

A smile crept to my lips as I began to drift, exhaustion taking hold of my battered body even as my mind clung to irony. It was amusing how little faith my family had in me. As if I hadn't planned every second, every beat of the show, every movement of the scarf, down to the moment I let myself vanish through the stage. They saw foolishness, a girl with a death wish.

I saw the opening move in a story that belonged, for once, to me.

IX. THE SECRET

Claude

My mouth tasted of ash.

I fumbled upright in bed, the wool blanket clinging to my legs with damp insistence. My shirt twisted in the night, the collar stiff and crusted to my skin. I peeled it away, wincing at the flare of pain despite the sweat drenching me from head to toe. Turning to the mirror on my bedside table, I immediately fixated on the bruises covering my neck, purple fingerprints blooming beneath my jaw as if someone tried to strangle me in my sleep. As if *I* tried to strangle myself.

It took a moment for the rest of my room to take shape. Everything was cold and gray, the morning light slicing through the high windows in thin lines. My desk was a chaos of papers and half-melted candles, the scent of old wax mixed in with the lingering smoke from the fireplace. Quasimodo's carved bird was perched at the desk's fringes, its wings outstretched as if overseeing my ruin. I stared at it, willing myself to remember what came after the fire, after the crowd, after the scarf.

The scarf.

A tremor ran through me, sudden and absolute, as if I'd been doused with cold water. The scarf lay there, coiled in the bedsheets like a venomous serpent. It glimmered in the half-light, beads black as sin, silk stained dark from the rain, and—God help me—even after last night, it still smelled of lilac and smoke. I slept with it, or it slept with me. The distinction was as thin as the air in my lungs.

Snatching it up before my mind could fully process my actions, I fumbled, nearly dropping it. It was heavier than I remembered, and still damp, the beads clacking together as I tried to stuff it into the drawer of my nightstand. The color was obscene against the black of my nightclothes, a living wound against the pallor of the sheets. My hands wouldn't stop shaking. It took two tries to jam the drawer shut, and even then, an accusing corner of silk peeked out.

I stood there, panting, one palm braced on the desk, the other pressed to my chest as if I could slow the hammering of my heart by force. The room was cold, yet my skin burned as if I were feverish. The urge to vomit, to scream, to run was so strong I nearly crumpled to the floor. Instead I staggered to the window and flung it open, letting the winter air slap me in the face. The wind carried the memory of the market: wet stone, boiled chestnuts, the earthy smell the rain left behind. I closed my eyes, counting the seconds until my pulse steadied, then forced the window shut and turned to face the room.

The scarf wasn't alone in its indictment. My boots, caked with dried mud from the square, sat where I kicked them off. My cloak, still stinking of the city, of the market, lay spread on the floor. And there, tangled in the folds, was a single strand of hair: black as pitch, stubbornly clinging to the wool. I plucked it free, held it up to the light, and the world tilted beneath me.

I had to get rid of it. All of it. The evidence, the memory, the lingering poison in my blood. I snatched up the cloak, then the scarf from my drawer, bundled them together, and shoved both into the trunk at the foot of my bed. My hands moved with mechanical efficiency, burying the bundle under old vestments, linens, anything that might soak up the scent and the shame both. For good measure, I pressed the heel of my boot down on the trunk's lid, grinding it shut until the latch snapped in place. Only then did I let myself breathe. Once, twice, three times, eyes screwed shut, hands braced on bent knees.

It wasn't enough. Nothing would ever be enough.

I stood, wiped my palms on my thighs, and forced my face into something resembling composure. I couldn't afford to fall apart. Not now, not ever. The market would be crawling with guards by now. Father Laurent would want a full accounting before vespers. I needed to trim my hair, to clean the crusted blood from my neck, to find a way to explain the bruises without revealing the truth behind them. I needed to—

The door creaked open behind me. I spun, heart in my throat, but it was only Quasimodo, barefoot and silent, his red hair unkempt and his eyes so earnest it made my bones ache. He didn't knock because he didn't need to. He slipped into my room as if it were his own, blinking at the cold and the mess, then at me, his face soft with concern. He took in the chaos—the upturned chair, the open window, the bruises on my neck—and signed, *Are you sick?*

I shook my head, then nodded, then shook it again, unable to commit to either lie. *I'm fine,* I responded once my fingers could form the shapes. *Just a rough night.* I tried to smile, but the muscles in my face couldn't quite manage it.

Quasimodo watched me, then came closer, his hands moving in patient, precise arcs: *The guards are angry. Some say you helped start the riot. Is it true?* His brow furrowed, the question gentle but relentless.

Of course not, I signed back. Too quickly. *The crowd was restless before we even got there. You saw that.*

It was hard to see anything, which is why I'm asking you.

I shook my head before he even finished. *I just happened to be there. That's all.*

But The Embermage gave you her scarf. Quasimodo's eyes remained bright, yet confused. *You were wearing it on our way back.*

Shame and desperation threatened to drown me. I thought about denying it, to convince Quasimodo that he didn't remember correctly. But after everything I'd already done, I couldn't bear to add lying to my son—again—to my ever-growing list of sins. I looked at my hands, then at his, and signed back, *It didn't mean anything. I'm not in trouble, and neither are you.*

He didn't believe me, and I could see it in his face. Reaching for my wrist, he turned it over to examine the fresh marks—half-moons where my own nails bit deep. He looked up, eyes wide and kind, and signed, *You're hurt again.*

I jerked my hand back, cradling it against my chest. *It's nothing.* But the words fell flat in the cold, heavy air between us. Quasimodo's lips pressed together, the stubborn line of his jaw so like my own it made me want to crack open my mask, to sob in his arms. He stepped back, giving me space, but his eyes never left the marks on my wrist.

He signed, careful and slow, as if aware of how close I was to breaking: *You didn't give her the bird.*

I opened my mouth, closed it. My fingers hovered in the air, trembling. I willed myself to sign, even as my mind screamed at having hurt him. *I'm sorry,* I said, hands stiff and ugly. *I forgot the bird here.*

A beat passed. He studied me with that impossible gentleness, the kind that made me want to shrink into myself, to throw myself out the window—possibly both. I wanted to tell him the truth, the *whole* truth, wanted it so much it physically pained me, but couldn't. Not after the Sirots. Not after the scarf, the fire. Not with Father Laurent's letter still ringing in my ears.

Quasimodo's hands moved again, slower this time: *Will we go back?*

I shook my head. I tried to make it convincing, but he saw right through me. He always did.

His hands dropped to his sides, fingers curling and uncurling. He stared at me for a long moment, searching my face as if he could dig up the truth by sheer force of will. When he found nothing but my trembling silence, he nodded and slipped from the room, closing the door with a careful finality I'd never heard from him before. The sound of it echoed through the stone and marrow of the cathedral. The ache it left behind was a clean, perfect wound.

I slumped against the desk, arms shaking, and let myself unravel for a few seconds. The urge to run after him, to beg forgiveness, to confess everything, every failure, every moment of cowardice, was so strong I tripped over the chair chasing it. But what would I say? That I was obsessed with a woman I'd been ordered to destroy? That I let the Sirots vanish, and did nothing but wring my hands and make excuses? That I was no better than Laurent, than the new Captain, no matter how many nights I spent flagellating myself to sleep?

No. The only thing worse than lying to Quasimodo was burdening him with a truth he could not change.

I made myself presentable, or at least a passable imitation. My hands trembled as I buttoned my shirt, but I forced each through its hole with slow, deliberate patience. My collar wouldn't lie flat, so I tied a black scrap of cloth tightly enough to hide the bruises. I bound my chest with an extra layer, the linen stiff and unyielding, then shrugged into my overcoat, its weight a comfort and a punishment both. In the mirror, my face was drawn and pale, the blue of my eyes gone flat with exhaustion. I pressed my fingers to my cheeks, willing warmth into them, and practiced a smile sharp enough to draw blood.

It was almost enough.

As if on cue, Father Laurent's summons arrived as I finished lacing my boots. The knock was crisp, the messenger a child from the orphanage who lingered in the doorway, eyes wide and wary as if expecting me to strike him.

I took the folded note with a nod, read the single line—*Come at once, F.L.*—and crushed it in my fist before the boy could even leave the threshold. He watched me for a moment, then turned and scurried down the hall, his footsteps echoing as if they were a warning bell. Every corridor seemed longer than usual, the shadows in the cathedral stretching and curling, hungry for secrets. The incense from morning prayers still hung heavy in the air, clinging to the carved stone like a second skin. My eyes watered as I passed the high altar, the candles there flickering as if there were a draft. The nave was empty, but the hush wasn't peaceful. There was tension, strung tight as the wires in the choir loft, waiting to snap.

I reached Laurent's door and hesitated, knuckles hovering above the wood. Just beyond, I could hear the scrape of a pen, the slow, deliberate shuffling of parchment. I counted to five, then knocked. The pen stopped.

"Enter," came the reply. I obeyed.

Father Laurent's office was a reliquary of small cruelties: the desk perfectly squared to the room, the shelves lined with ledgers and bound sermons, the windows shuttered against even the thought of sunlight. He sat behind the desk, hands folded over a stack of reports, his face as blank as the stone saints on the west portal. He didn't stand, nor did he offer me a seat when I entered. There was no ceremony, no trace of warmth. He simply waited, eyes fixed on the page before him.

I stood in the center of the rug, hands clasped behind my back, and counted the seconds until he chose to look up. When he did, it was with the slow precision of a man who spent his entire life perfecting the art of discomfort—because he had. He regarded me with a level, unreadable gaze, then tapped his finger on the topmost report.

"Sit," he said. It wasn't a suggestion.

I did as I was told, lowering myself onto the narrow wooden chair that faced his desk. The seat was too low, designed to make even the tallest man feel childlike. I folded my hands in my lap, willing myself to be still. The bruises on my neck throbbed in time with my pulse.

Father Laurent let the silence linger. Then, with a single motion, he slid the stack of papers across the desk to rest directly before me.

"Do you know what this is?" he asked.

I glanced down. The top page was an incident log, written in Father Laurent's own precise, looping hand. The word MARKET was underlined twice, the ink bold and black, the rest of the page a neat grid of times and names and brief, damning notes. I recognized several of the names, all market regulars, most of them harmless, some not even mages. My own name, FROLLO, was circled in red at the bottom of the sheet.

I didn't bother feigning ignorance. "Reports from last night?"

Laurent's lips twitched, the barest ghost of a smile. "You were seen at the market during the disturbance, you and your son. Several reliable witnesses place you at the center of the crowd, near the stage. Others say you intervened on behalf of the performer."

I kept my face still. "I attempted to disperse the crowd before it turned violent. That is my duty."

Laurent's gaze sharpened. "And yet, rather than assist the guard, you fled." He let the implication hang, then turned a page. "You know the Bishop expects a full accounting. He isn't pleased."

The urge to rub my throat was overwhelming, but I gripped my knees instead. "There was confusion. The performer—she incited the crowd, then vanished. I saw no reason to pursue when the guards had everything under control."

Father Laurent's smile remained fixed, but his eyes glittered with something sharp and ugly. "*Everything under control*," he repeated, as if trying out the taste of it. "Is that why three guards are in the infirmary with burns? Or why the crowd nearly tore apart the Captain's men before the performer disappeared? Is that your assessment of 'under control'?"

I forced myself to meet his gaze. "The guards overreacted. They charged the stage before anyone gave an order, and the crowd panicked. I did what I could to de-escalate the situation."

Laurent considered me, drumming his fingers on the desk. "There are other reports. Not from the guards, but from the market itself. Several witnesses claim you were seen in... rather close proximity to the performer. Some say you exchanged words. Some say you even—" he paused, eyes flicking to my neck, "—*touched* her."

I willed myself not to move. "Rumor and hysteria. You know how these stories spread."

He leaned back, folding his hands. "If it's just rumor, you have nothing to fear. But the Bishop is already assembling a commission. Captain Phoebus is demanding to interview you himself. He believes you're collaborating with her," he finished, voice low and deliberate. "He's convinced you're compromised."

I almost laughed. "He's new," I said, letting the contempt bleed through. "He'll learn before long the city runs on gossip, not fact."

Laurent's eyes narrowed. "The Bishop does not share your optimism. He's ordered a full inquiry. Every witness, every guard, every priest who so much as set foot in the square last night is to be interviewed. You'll be the first."

There was a note of satisfaction in his voice, a quiet pleasure in seeing me cornered. For a moment, I considered what it would feel like to simply confess: to pour out the entire mess, the hunger, the obsession, the way her hands felt on my skin—let it all tumble forth and watch the Church recoil in horror. It would be almost worth it to see their faces.

But I had not survived this long by surrendering before the knives were even drawn.

I straightened my spine and fixed Father Laurent with a look as cold as the morning air. "Let them question me," I said. "I have nothing to hide."

"Don't be foolish," he snapped, the first crack in his composure all morning. "You know what's at stake. You know as well as I do that the Bishop doesn't want a scandal. If Phoebus gets what he wants, you'll be stripped of your post and tried before the city. And that's if you're *lucky*."

There it was—laid out, clinical and clean, the way Laurent always preferred his threats. I almost admired the efficiency of it. "What do you want from me?"

He tapped the reports again. "I want you to tell me the truth. I want you to admit what you did last night, so I can manage the damage before it spreads." He leaned forward, the light catching on the hard ridge of his cheekbone. "I need to know where your loyalties lie, Claude."

The old ache in my chest flared, but I kept my face blank. "With the Church. With Paris."

"That's what I thought. And for that reason, I have already taken the liberty of resolving this… unfortunate business."

I remained silent, my hands gripping my knees beneath the desk. I didn't understand.

"A public inquiry would be a messy, inconvenient affair," he continued, steepling his fingers. "An embarrassment for the Bishop. It is better for everyone if the matter is handled with discretion. I have already spoken with Captain Phoebus and the Bishop. The official report will state that the performer used a powerful illusion glamour to incite the crowd, and that you were merely a victim of the chaos. The inquiry, therefore, is no longer necessary."

A wave of relief so profound it was sickening washed over me.

The immediate threat—the interviews, the trial—was gone.

"You will, of course, corroborate this version of events if asked," Laurent said, his voice smooth as poison. "And from now on, any… *erratic impulses*… you will bring to me before you act upon them. I have vouched for your loyalty, Claude. Do not make me regret my generosity."

The relief curdled into a cold, suffocating dread. The threat of the inquiry was gone, but it had been replaced by a cage. He had not freed me. He had simply shortened my leash until it was a collar. The silence stretched, filling the room with the weight of what he wasn't saying. I could see the calculation flicker behind his eyes, the subtle readjustment of tactics. Laurent didn't believe in confession as salvation. He believed in the theater of it, the leverage, the slow bleed of vulnerability. I recognized the game because I learned it from him.

"You will also be at vespers tonight," he added, his gaze flicking to the bruises on my neck. "And every night. A show of your renewed commitment is… expected."

"Yes, Father," I whispered. The words felt like stones in my throat.

He gave a small, satisfied nod, the ghost of a smirk finally reaching his lips. He had won. He had laid out the terms of my surrender, and I had accepted without a fight.

He waved a hand, a final, absolute dismissal. "Go."

The corridor outside was colder than before, every step echoing in my bones. I walked without thinking, the meeting replaying in my head, each memory a fragment of a threat or warning. Drifting down the length of the nave, the hollow of the church threatened to swallow me whole. I wanted to let it, to surrender, to leave nothing behind but a neat, bloodless shell. I was at the crossing—where the transept met the nave, the heart of the cathedral—when an all-too-familiar silhouette came into view.

Mercedes stood in the shadow of a pillar, arms folded, hair pulled back beneath a simple headscarf. She wore the same blue as always, a color that should have been soft, yet it reflected off the stained glass. I tried to pass without acknowledging her, but she stepped into my path, her movement precise and intentional.

"Claude," she said, voice low. "You look like shit."

I didn't bother to scold her for swearing. "You always did prefer honesty to courtesy."

"Where the hell were you last night?" she demanded, eyes bright and burning. "I know I left upset, but I just needed a moment to compose myself. When I came back, you were gone."

I shrugged, feigning nonchalance. "I was summoned by Laurent. I spent most of the evening answering questions about the market. There's an inquiry. You'll be called, too, I expect."

She didn't flinch. She just watched me, her gaze flicking to the bruises at my throat and then back to my eyes. "You're a terrible liar," she snapped. "Try again."

I opened my mouth, but she cut me off with a shake of her head. "No. Don't bother. I *know* where you went. I *saw* the way you looked at her." She paused, adding, "You're not the only one with business in the market, Claude. That scarf—where'd you put it?"

My voice vanished. Mercedes took a step closer, the distance between us nearly nonexistent. For a moment, I thought she might hit me, or kiss me, or do both at once—instead, she reached up and touched her own jaw, the faintest bruise visible just below the cheekbone. It was not an accusation; rather, a reminder to both of us.

"I'm sorry," I said, and I meant it. "I—"

She stopped me with a look, and when she spoke again, she didn't raise her voice. "You always want to make it about you, Claude." Her words weren't cruel, just tired. "You think you're the only one who carries the weight of this hurt and shame." Her eyes flicked to the bruises on my neck, then to where my hands trembled in the sleeves of my coat. "Let me make it easy for you—for both of us," she added, voice dropping so low it barely carried above the stillness of the church. "If you're so determined to ruin yourself, fine. I won't stop you. But I won't let you ruin me, too."

She stepped sideways, her shoulder brushing mine, and in that brief contact I felt the ghost of the old comfort, the warmth that used to live between us. It lasted less than a breath. Then she was gone, her footsteps echoing down the nave, the blue of her shawl swallowed by the cold, indifferent light. I stood there, rooted, unable to move, until the last trace of her vanished into shadow.

I waited a full minute before I could trust my legs to carry me forward, my hands shaking all the while. I made it to the end of the nave, then ducked into the first side corridor and braced my shoulder against the wall, trying and failing to steady my ragged breaths. The silence was deafening, a tomb for every failed prayer I'd ever uttered.

I pressed my palms to my eyes until I saw stars.

When I finally surfaced, I went straight to my quarters, locking the door behind me with shaking hands. The chamber was cold and bleak, the only color that obscene sliver of violet still peeking from the trunk at the foot of my bed. The sight of it made my skin crawl. I wanted to burn it, to salt the earth where it lay, to erase the memory of her hands on my throat and the impossible fire in her eyes.

I yanked the scarf free, fingers digging into the silk until the beads bit into my knuckles. The scent of lilac and smoke was fainter now, but still there, stubborn as sin. My first instinct was to tear it apart with my teeth, to rip every bead from the thread and scatter them out the window. Instead, I stumbled to the fireplace, knelt on the rough stone, and jammed the scarf deep into the embers.

The fire caught slowly, as if unwilling. The silk smoldered, beads popping one by one in the heat, each tiny explosion sending a sharp, bitter tang into the air. As the violet silk curled to black, I saw her face: not in the flames, but behind my eyelids, as if my mind refused to let me be rid of her. The Embermage. Her mouth curled in that impossible, crooked smile; her eyes alive, that defiant green. I remembered the feel of her hand at my jaw, the warmth of her breath as she leaned in, the connection that passed between us in a heartbeat. I remembered the way she looked at me—*really* looked, as if I were not just a man or a monster, but something worth saving, or at least someone worth sparing.

The memory hit so hard I doubled over, knuckles white where I gripped the edge of the hearth. I couldn't breathe. I couldn't think. The world spun, the firelight flickering across the stone, and for one terrifying instant, I wanted nothing more than to throw myself into the flames alongside the scarf, to let it burn me down to bone and ash.

With a sound halfway between a sob and a curse, I reached into the fire and snatched the scarf back—burning my palm, barely feeling it through the numbness—and cradled it to my chest, choking on a sound I'd never made before. Something between a gasp and a sob, but neither. The silk stuck to my skin, the edge scorched but not yet consumed, the beads blistering-hot even through my calloused fingers. I collapsed back onto the stone, clutching it, rocking like a child, letting the smoke sting my eyes until I was certain the tears would never stop.

I couldn't do it. I couldn't destroy the one thing that proved she touched me, seen me, that any of it had been real.

Pressing the scarf to my face, I breathed in the ghost of her perfume, and for a moment it was as if she knelt beside me, hands gentle at my neck, mouth at my ear, whispering absolution I knew I'd never deserve. The pain in my palm was a pinprick compared to the ache in my chest. I couldn't destroy it, then—but neither could I hide it. I couldn't risk it being found or anyone knowing who I truly was, what I'd *done*.

Staggering back, I cradled my burned palm, the smell of scorched silk still curling through the room. I would keep the scarf on my person, but I wouldn't acknowledge it again. I wouldn't let myself think of her—not the woman, not the magic, not the way she looked at me like I was the only soul in the world worth the trouble. I would forget. I would bury it all. If I couldn't, I would at least pretend, for Quasimodo's sake, for the Church's, for my own.

I wiped my eyes with the back of my hand. The skin was red and blistered, the pain radiating up my wrist with each heartbeat. I wrapped my injured hand in linen, careful and slow, then sat on the edge of the bed, clutching the scarf in my opposite fist and forcing myself to breathe until the world steadied.

As I stared out the window at the late afternoon light, the truth came freely: I would survive this, for I survived far worse. Just as Laurent had ordered, I would go back to who I was before, to the hollow silence, to the familiar comfort of the shadows and the blackness, to the safety of my own damnation. I would perform my duties, I would care for my son, and I would confess my sins—all of them, except the one that mattered. I would bury the memory of her touch, her scent, her impossible fire. I would go back to being a ghost in my own life, a spectre in the halls of the cathedral, unseen and untouched. It was the only way to keep my sanity, to keep Laurent's leash from tightening any more than it already had.

But there was a final truth, one I could not deny any more than I could deny the existence of my God—I had been *seen*. Against my will, or perhaps because I willed it hardly mattered. For a cathartic, freeing moment, I knew the warmth of light.

The dark, familiar as it was, would never again be enough.

AUTHOR'S NOTE

The Psalm of Ashen Silk is a story that has lived in my head for years. I always knew there was a beginning to Claude and Esmeralda's love story—specifically, the handing off of the scarf—but I never imagined that one little scene could be expanded into a complete tale of its own.

The last couple of years have been a whirlwind of wonderful life changes for me: from getting engaged and married, to buying our first home, and making it our own. Amidst all the beautiful chaos, finding the quiet moments to write has been a challenge. Coming back to Claude and Esmeralda's world with this novella felt like coming home. *Psalm* was the perfect project to reignite my passion and dive back into the lives of these characters I love so dearly.

This is just the beginning of their journey, and I am so grateful you're here for it. I can't wait to share even more of their story with you.

Whether this was your first visit to gothic Paris or a return trip, there's more of Claude and Esmeralda's story to discover.

New to the series? Their story continues in the full-length novel…

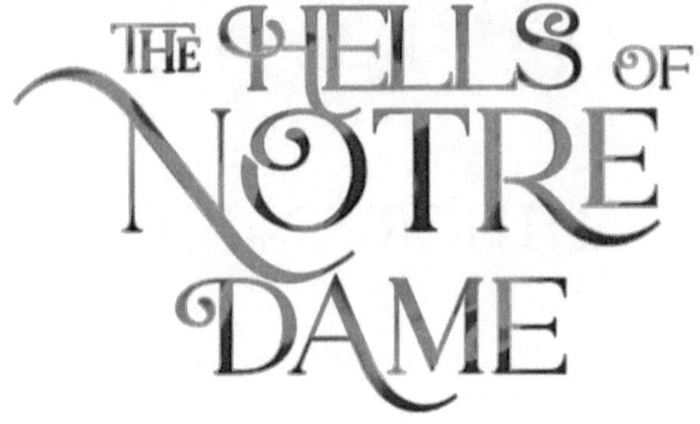

Months have passed. Claude, now trapped under the watchful eye of the Church, desperately clings to the secret of the violet scarf she keeps hidden against her skin. Esmeralda, bound by a sacred promise to her family that she intends to break, prepares for her final, dangerous move. When a new threat emerges from the shadows of the cathedral, their two worlds are set on a collision course that will either save them or burn them both to ash.

Keep reading for the first chapter!

Already read *The Hells of Notre Dame* and came back for the beginning?

First of all, thank you! I'm so glad you're here. And second, I have something special for you.

I have exclusive bonus chapters from *The Hells of Notre Dame*—including extra steamy scenes and different points of view—that are available *only* to my newsletter subscribers. It's my way of saying thank you for being such a wonderful part of this community.

Claim your bonus content here:

https://rldavennor.com/newsletter

I. THE SCARF

Claude

"Ave, María, grátia plena, Dóminus tecum."

Hail Mary, indeed. I had survived another week, gotten through another Friday, and at last, my mask could begin to slip without consequence. It was the moment I looked forward to the most: the blessed quiet following Vespers and the evening Mass where it was only me and Saint Mary. I had recited her prayer every dusk since I was old enough to speak, and as always, I went slowly, placing weight on every sacred word.

"Benedicta tu in muliéribus, et benedíctus fructus ventris tui, Iesus."

I didn't dare lift my head from where it rested atop my clasped hands and instead marveled at the gorgeous array of colors painting the otherwise drab stone floor. Notre Dame was breathtaking at sunset, when the stained glass sang for a final time before going dormant for the night.

A smile crept to my lips at the thought, because tonight, I'd be long gone by the time darkness fell.

But I couldn't so much as stand until I finished my prayer, and that would never happen unless I stilled my mind and focused. Inhaling deeply, I recited the final line, willing Saint Mary to sense my devotion.

"Sancta María, Mater Dei, ora pro nobis peccatoribus nunc et in hora mortis nostrae."

On any other night, here was the part I would say *amen*. I would rise, lock up my office, and meet Quasimodo upstairs, where we would have dinner, talk, and read before retiring to our rooms for the evening.

But today was Friday, the night we visited a place where I needed Saint Mary's strength more than any other. I couldn't end my prayer before asking for her blessing, not if I had any hope of keeping my wits about me. Here, I may be Archdeacon of Notre Dame, but there, I became a woman stripped down to my most primal urges. And those urges wanted nothing but *her*.

Closing my eyes, I squeezed my hands together so hard they hurt. My voice came out raspy and hoarse, and the words garbled due to the excess saliva pooling in my mouth. "Blessed Virgin, you know of the sin that tempts me." It had far more than tempted me—I had shattered my vow of celibacy all to Hell, acting upon my impure urges more times than I could count—but I shoved the ugly truth aside. "Forgive me. Break these chains that bind me. Cleanse my heart and soul, and free me from this ceaseless torment."

Said torment's beautiful face flashed in my mind. With luscious raven curls, rich umber skin, and eyes like emeralds, it was little wonder The Embermage had haunted my dreams these past months, but acknowledging her beauty didn't make the burden any easier to bear. I couldn't close my eyes without picturing the near-constant sheen of sweat clinging to flesh whose gleaming silver undertones were revealed only in moonlight, couldn't place my hand anywhere on my body without it wanting to migrate between my legs. The punishing hold she had over me was as maddening as it was intoxicating... but one way or another, it ended tonight.

One final visit to the street faire in which The Embermage regularly performed. Yes, that was what I needed to get her out of my system—to watch her dance among the flames one last time, to meet her gaze in a sea of hundreds, to look and marvel, but never touch. Never, *ever* touch, not even if she begged me to.

But God, envisioning The Embermage on her knees, pleading for—

"Protect me, Mother Mary, as you protected your son, and I will do the same for mine," I blurted out, horrified at where my thoughts had strayed. That was what I needed to remember, why I needed to keep myself pure. If for no one or nothing else, I needed to think of Quasimodo, my son and my responsibility. No more sneaking around with Mercedes, no more lusting after The Embermage, and after tonight, no more visits to the faire. Ever. I'd accepted my place at Notre Dame for a reason, and it was high time I began living what I preached. It was one thing to damn myself to the pits of Hell, and entirely another to drag my innocent son along with me.

Tonight it was, then. But no more.

"In the name of the Father, and of the Son, and of the Holy Spirit," I whispered solemnly, unclasping my hands to make the sign of the cross, "Amen."

When I stood, I immediately felt lighter. Freer. The ever-present ache in my chest lifted as I turned toward Saint Mary's likeness depicted in stained glass, and a familiar calm washed over me the moment our gazes locked. There was a reason I prayed to Saint Mary rather than God in the evenings. I loved Him dearly, but as a fellow mother, Saint Mary understood me in a way He simply never could. Sunlight filtered through the dazzling display, bathing me in a rainbow of color and informing me of a single truth: even after all these years, despite all my sins and flaws, a higher power still watched over and protected me. No matter what vitriol my peers in the clergy spouted about people like me, to some higher power, I was accepted. I was enough. Grateful tears welled in my eyes, because whether it was Saint Mary's or God's doing hardly mattered. I'd accept whomever's blessing I could get.

After regaining my composure and collecting my prayer cushion from the floor, I made the short walk back to my office. The door was closed, which surprised me only because the maids were usually here cleaning by now, but it didn't upset me—not when it meant I'd have even more quiet time to myself. I loved Quasimodo dearly, but given that we were about to spend an entire evening together, I fully intended to wait until the designated time to meet him, and not a moment sooner. He wouldn't expect me for another fifteen minutes.

Perfect.

I closed and locked the door before placing the cushion on my desk. Leaning my palms against the cool wood, I scrutinized its surface. Everything was exactly as I'd left it: neat, orderly, and organized, all yet another indication no one had been in here, and that I was alone. Truly alone, especially now that I'd begged forgiveness for my immortal soul. The afterglow of my prayer, and presumably God's watchful eye, had faded.

What I chose to do next would be for me and me alone to know.

Heart pounding, I reached within the neck of my robe and pulled out my prize, carefully and gently so as not to tear the sheer fabric. A scarf, but not just any scarf. It had once belonged to *her.*

I recalled the night I'd acquired it in exquisite detail. I'm still not sure what possessed me to stand so near the stage, but it was an inexplicable pull I didn't bother to fight, and Quasimodo was thrilled to be in the front row. Our proximity hadn't escaped The Embermage's attention. About halfway through her performance, she'd leaned down, yanked the scarf from her neck, and wrapped it around mine, pulling our faces so close I could have pulled back my hood and kissed her. For the rest of my life, I'd regret that I hadn't.

But as quickly as it happened, the moment shattered, leaving me breathless and with the scarf still draped over my shoulders. It was a beautiful, delicate thing, and its violet fabric smelled of smoke and the faintest hint of lilac. As my most treasured possession, the scarf hadn't left my person since the moment I'd acquired it, but not only because I couldn't let anyone else find it.

I may be a holy woman, but I sure as hell wasn't a saint.

My free hand had already drifted below my waist to gather up my vestments. There were quite a few layers to get through, but my practiced fingers made short work of them, fueled by the need pulsing between my thighs. Just my undergarments stood in the way now, and then—

"Did you two finally fuck?"

I nearly screamed. With trembling, careless hands, I shoved the scarf back into its prison and yanked down my robe before whirling around, both surprised and somehow not at all to see a red-haired woman leaning against the far wall. Though half-bathed in shadow, it was easy to make out the sea of freckles dotting her porcelain skin, though her maid's uniform concealed that they extended down her shoulders all the way to her hands, as well as other places I'd seen more times than I could count. Arms crossed, she raised an eyebrow, clearly not planning on saying anything else until I did.

"Mercedes." Her name came out more breathless than I intended. I wish I could have attributed that to her use of profanity, but if I allowed her crassness to bother me, we'd never be able to have anything resembling a civilized conversation. "The door was locked."

"Since when has that ever stopped me?"

Like the other maids, Mercedes had keys to just about everywhere, but last I was aware, that wasn't meant to include my office—for good reason. "What the hell are you doing here?"

She held my gaze, her expression impassive. "Watch your tongue. Father Laurent wouldn't like it. Me, on the other hand..."

"Stop that."

"Stop what?"

"Don't be coy," I snapped, having regained my composure. "You know precisely what you're doing."

"Do I?" Mercedes cocked her head. "I'm not sure I'd say that, as it's not yet had the desired effect."

I bit back a groan and instead bit my tongue. *Lord, give me strength.* This woman knew precisely how to push my buttons, and I hadn't yet decided if it was infuriating or thrilling, especially given what she'd interrupted. It took every ounce of energy I possessed to rein in my impulses, but despite my efforts, my defenses were rapidly crumbling. "You're not supposed to be here."

"You're not supposed to have that scarf."

That smart little mouth of hers was going to be the death of me. "Why *are* you here?"

"What are you doing with that scarf?"

"Answer the question."

"Make me."

My body reacted before my mind caught up. One moment I was at my desk, and the next, I undid weeks of good behavior, and my hand was around Mercedes's throat. She gasped the moment I touched her, but not in pain—I knew the difference intimately well. The corners of her mouth twitched up, hinting at a smile, and her hips bucked against mine, seeking friction rather than escape. I gathered both her wrists in my free hand before raising them above her head, shifting my weight forward, and tilting her chin up at a near-harsh angle, effectively immobilizing her against the wall. She moaned then, soft and restrained, but given that my own constraint had already snapped, I wasn't sure what to feel. Shame? Regret? Disgust?

Any of them would have been appropriate, because everything about what I had just done was wrong. A *sin*. My silver hair may be cropped as short as the rest of the clergy, my breasts bound for most of my waking hours, and my garb identical to my male counterparts, but beneath the modifications I found necessary to better serve my church and my God, I was every bit as womanly as Mercedes. Both nature and my religion dictated that I should find men appealing… or ideally, no one at all, given my vows.

But I couldn't deny my attraction to other women any more than I could deny my God, and my sexual preferences were a festering wound I'd wrestled with my entire life. By day, I was a devout, pious Catholic, performing my duties as Archdeacon and far more whenever necessary, but by night, I sinned, recklessly pursuing pleasures of the flesh. My lust was overpowering and often insatiable. I'd even been known to have multiple women in the same night and still be left wanting more… though when Mercedes was willing and available, other partners were rarely necessary. She had a sexual appetite to rival mine, one of the many things I found appealing about her.

And though I'd never admit it aloud, *God*, I'd missed her. Avoiding her had been pure torture, and now that she was here and my hands were on her, I couldn't resist indulging. "Is this what you wanted?" I breathed against her cheek, lightly nipping at her earlobe. It may have been weeks since I'd touched her—or anyone—but I hadn't forgotten how to handle a woman, nor the games Mercedes liked to play. "To be at my mercy? I bet you'll do anything I ask so long as it ends with my hand up your skirt."

"I will." Her response was more a whine than anything else, and she bucked her hips against mine before meeting my gaze. "Please, Claude. It's been so long."

She was right about that, and I couldn't remember the last time we'd slept together or even come close. Just four months ago, Mercedes and I couldn't go more than twenty-four hours without undressing one another, but circumstances had changed, especially after we'd nearly been caught one too many times. With Mercedes already on thin ice given her past and me unwilling to risk endangering my son, we'd agreed to end the relationship that had never truly been one to begin with, and return to being friends without benefits.

But there was more to it than that, a truth we had yet to acknowledge aloud. Around that same time was when I began visiting the street faire and participating in its festivities every Friday night. It had started innocently enough with my sole intention being to bring a smile to Quasimodo's face, but one look at *her* and it became anything but. The Embermage and her dazzling performances had enchanted me mind and soul, but I wanted and needed far more. She had become an addiction, a compulsion overshadowing my desire for anyone and anything else. Mercedes knew me well enough to notice all of it—my change in demeanor, and certainly where I'd been going—she'd just kept her mouth shut.

Until now, apparently, because she was still giving me an

identical look to when she'd first questioned the scarf. A flash of anger had me gripping her throat slightly tighter. She knew damn well why I'd been avoiding her, but if she wanted me to say it, she would leave here disappointed.

And what had she said? Right—that it had been a while. "It has, and you know why."

"No, I don't," Mercedes shot back, voice slightly hoarse. "If we need to be careful, then let's be more careful. If you no longer want me, just say so. But it's neither of those things. You're rejecting me for someone else. For *her*."

I almost flinched at both the pain in Mercedes's voice and her mention of The Embermage. "I'm not rejecting you, and there *is* no one else."

"Then fuck me."

I swallowed the sudden lump that had formed in my throat. "I… I can't."

"See?" Mercedes's eyes glistened in a way that suggested she was about to claw my eyes out or cry; perhaps both. "Rejection."

"That's not rejection. I said I can't, not that I won't."

"Then why won't you? Are you two exclusive?"

"I'm never exclusive."

"Then, does her cunt truly taste that much better than mine?"

Christ, she was getting loud. "Keep your voice down—"

"Is she prettier than me?"

"Of course not."

"Do you love her?"

Oh, God—the 'L' word, the one I loathed above all others, and the one Mercedes knew better than to utter. My control snapped yet again, and for the second time, my body took over without conscious or rational thought. Stepping aside, I released Mercedes's throat to snatch the nape of her neck, walk her forward, and bend her over my desk. I ignored her startled yelp as I tangled one hand in her auburn curls, forcing her head up, and only barely resisted the urge to smack her rounded bottom. She more than deserved it for what she'd insinuated.

"I love no one but my God and my son, in that order. Is that clear?"

"Yes."

"Yes, who?" I tightened my already punishing grip on her hair.

"Yes, Mis— I mean, Archdeacon Frollo."

"Good." Before I could give in to any more of my sinful urges, I stepped away, leaving Mercedes a breathless, trembling mess as I slumped against the far wall, sinking to my knees. My heart was racing, and my hands shook when I lifted them to where I could examine them. Making the sign of the cross didn't help ease the panic, nor did trying to picture Saint Mary's likeness just down the hall. An icy chill crept over my skin as the reality of what I'd just done set in. I had touched a woman in a sexual manner *again*, and very well may have bedded her if I wasn't already lusting after another. I remained captive to these urges, these cravings, this torment that refused to leave me alone, and had no end in sight.

What if God had been watching us just now and I'd failed Him? What if my very existence was a sin, an abomination, a mistake, and that everything my colleagues whispered about me was true? What if no amount of penance would ever be enough? What if my immortal soul was already damned straight to Hell?

"Are you all right?" Mercedes asked quietly, and only then did I realize I'd been raking my nails over my arms with such violence that there was a bit of blood. I yanked down my sleeves and lifted my head, only for another wave of shame to wash over me when I took in the sight of Mercedes, her disheveled hair and flushed cheeks. I should be asking if *she* was all right, but I didn't move or speak at first, focusing instead on regulating my breathing and keeping my pulse steady. I was no stranger to panic attacks, but it had been over a year since I'd had one in the presence of anyone else. The fact that I'd had one here and now, less than an hour before—

"Claude?" Though she remained where I left her, Mercedes spoke my name again, her tone firm enough to tear me from my rapidly spiraling thoughts. "Tell me what's going on."

"No." I pressed my lips together as I shot her a glare. She knew better than to order me around. "I'm fine."

Mercedes snorted. "Like hell you are."

My breath still came in heavy pants as she closed the distance between us, leaning down to sit beside me. I didn't protest as her fingers entwined with mine. Both reassuring and grounding, the gentleness of it felt far better than I wanted to admit.

"I'm sorry." She paused, her gaze slipping to the floor. "I shouldn't have pushed you like that."

"You shouldn't have asked me if I loved her," I said, low and almost more to myself than her. Love was… a complicated thing. I didn't want it anywhere near the women in my life, because ultimately, it was a weakness. And of all the things I couldn't afford to be, weak was at the very top of that list. Let it show, and Notre Dame would eat me alive even more than it already had.

"I shouldn't have," Mercedes agreed, "but I'm your friend, I miss you, and I worry about you. It's not just me you've been avoiding, and people are starting to notice. You haven't been yourself for months, Claude. Not since—"

"Don't."

She bit her lip and shook her head, causing her red curls to tumble over her shoulders. Despite how irritated I was with her, I reached out and tucked the runaway strands back behind her ear. Mercedes leaned into my touch, covering my hand with one of hers to keep it in place on her cheek. "I know I can't stop you from going to see her, and I won't try. But can you blame me for worrying? It's dangerous out there, and if you were caught, especially with what she…" Her voice trailed off when I shot her another glare. "Just… be careful, all right? And remember that you have people within these very walls who love you."

I chuckled darkly. "At Notre Dame? Besides Quasimodo, the only person with any love for me is you."

Only when I felt Mercedes's breaths on my neck did it register how close we were. She had shifted so she was nearly in my lap, and at some point, I must have turned so that I was fully facing her. My hand remained on her cheek when she lifted her gaze to mine, and I didn't miss the way it had been previously fixated on my lips.

"Mercedes…"

"Please," she whispered, so softly I barely heard her. "I know your rule. But I don't want to leave this room without having kissed you at least once."

The pain in her voice twisted my stomach into knots. Mercedes was far from the only sexual partner I'd confused and hurt over the strange fact that of all the things I was willing to do in bed, I drew the line at kissing. They all followed the same train of thought: how could I possibly have an issue with another woman's lips on mine when I was perfectly comfortable with lips touching any other part of my body? That was precisely it, though—the intimacy of such an act. And much like love, intimacy was something I avoided at all costs.

But Mercedes… oh, my Mercedes. I'd wanted to kiss her since I'd first laid eyes on her gorgeous auburn locks all those years ago. Like me, she'd lived and worked in Notre Dame for most of her life, and for that reason alone there had been an instant connection between us; completely platonic at first but one that rapidly grew into something more. She had been everything I'd ever needed her to be: my friend, my confidant, my colleague, and eventually the closest thing I'd ever had to a lover. Much as I wanted to keep up my stony façade, I couldn't deny the depth of our unique bond.

I certainly couldn't deny her now.

Mercedes leaned forward slowly, giving me ample opportunity to pull away or tell her no. When I did neither, she moaned before closing the remaining distance between us, tentatively pressing her lips to mine. Soft yet desperate, her kiss was far more innocent than I had expected, and it sent a shiver down my spine that kept me rooted in place. It had been so long since I'd been kissed, let alone kissed like this, that neither my body nor mind knew what to make of it.

But to my surprise, it was over as quickly as it started, and Mercedes all but ripped herself from me. Without another word or glance, she rose, pausing briefly to fix her hair and skirt, departing my office before I could so much as blurt out whether I'd done something wrong. I tried to ignore the way my heart ached, or at least not flinch when the door clicked shut, but Mercedes's unspoken message was loud and clear. Her kiss wasn't intended to be a comfort, hopeful, or even sad.

It was simply goodbye.

The Hells of Notre Dame **is available now, and you can get all formats, including signed copies, directly from the author below:**

https://rldavennor.com/products/the-hells-of-notre-dame

ABOUT THE AUTHOR

Raelynn Davennor (she/they) writes fantasy romance and fairytale retellings—usually of the darker variety—and is the author of the Curses of Never and The Phantom of Notre Dame series, both of which became viral BookTok hits. She is known for her diverse and morally complex characters, as well as her ability to craft heart-wrenching plots that explore heavy themes. While she is a firm believer that light cannot be fully appreciated without first traveling through heaps of darkness, Raelynn always ensures that her characters find their well-deserved happily ever afters—especially the LGBTQ+ ones. When not obsessing over her latest idea, she enjoys pampering her menagerie of pets and pretending she isn't an adult.

Her home base is https://rldavennor.com where you'll find more information, her newsletter, and links to social media.